"Get out!" he s

I shook my head

There was the s
and I glanced that way,
the archway to the entry hall, a man with a
cauliflower ear and a dimly familiar face.

"Trouble, Ricky?" the big man asked quietly.

I remembered him then, a former local wrestler
who had played bit parts as a heavy in a host of *B*
pictures.

"No trouble, George. Mr. Callahan is leaving."

"You're leaving," George Parkas said from the
doorway.

"Go away," I told him. "You're big but you're
old and you were never much. Go away before you
are forced to make an ass of yourself."

"I'll get the door," Rivali said, and started to
leave the room as George leaned forward and
reached for me.

My stout right leg came up, and I braced my
back into the davenport as I let George have it . . .

∾∾∾∾∾∾∾∾∾∾∾∾∾∾∾∾∾∾∾∾∾∾∾∾∾∾∾∾∾∾∾∾∾∾∾∾

Praise for William Campbell Gault

"Gault writes with passion, beauty . . . which has
previously been found only in Raymond
Chandler."

—*Los Angeles Daily News*

"The best news in recent years for mystery readers
is the return of William Campbell Gault."

—*Atlanta Journal & Constitution*

"Mr. Gault has written many other crime novels,
and sorry am I not to have discovered him before
now."

—*Best Sellers*

VEIN OF VIOLENCE

William Campbell Gault

CHARTER BOOKS, NEW YORK

This Charter Book contains the complete
text of the original edition.
It has been completely reset in a typeface
designed for easy reading, and was printed
from new film.

VEIN OF VIOLENCE

A Charter Book / published by arrangement with
the author

PRINTING HISTORY
Simon & Schuster edition published 1961
Award Books edition/February 1965
Charter edition/February 1988

ISBN: 1-55773-000-8

Charter Books are published by The Berkley Publishing Group,
200 Madison Avenue, New York, New York 10016.
The name "Charter" and the "C" logo are trademarks
belonging to Charter Communications, Inc.

PRINTED IN THE UNITED STATES OF AMERICA

10   9   8   7   6   5   4   3   2   1

For Mary Shirvanian

✠✠✠✠✠✠✠✠✠✠✠✠✠ *ONE* ✠✠✠✠✠✠✠✠✠✠✠✠✠✠

JAN, ALONE, IS usually more woman than an ordinary man can cope with, unreasonably mercurial, occasionally snobbish and always vocal. Jan in tandem with my Aunt Sheila is enough to make all sane citizens head for the cyclone cellars.

My Aunt Sheila is skinny and long-legged, with a firm bust for her age and a great appeal for men of money and appetite. She claims to be thirty-seven, but I happen to know she's forty-three. She has been married three times, courted often and conned never. Too many grass widows are overwhelmed with the *appearance* of wealth in a prospect; Aunt Sheila knows how to get a credit report.

Well, anyway, she had been living rather quietly in La Jolla for a couple of years, an area as alien to her temperament as any I could imagine. Even Pasadena is livelier than La Jolla.

And at a party up there one fine spring evening, she ran into Homer Gallup. Now what the hell Homer was doing in La Jolla is a question that will probably bother anthropologists for another century.

Because Homer is a Texan, and almost exactly in the stereotyped tradition of the moneyed Texan, big, bluff and vocal. La Jolla is not hospitable to the type.

I met him for the first time on a smog-saturated April

morning in my office. I was sitting there moodily, balancing my accounts receivable against my accounts payable, a sad reckoning.

The door to the hall was open and Aunt Sheila's voice has remarkable carrying power. I heard her say, "It's right along here somewhere, cheap little office— Poor Brock, he hasn't a smidgen of business sense. Ah, here it is!"

And she was standing in the open doorway, tall and trim and dressed in a light-yellow linen sheath. Her hair was more blond than orange this year.

"Brock, baby—!" she squealed, and charged me.

I stood up, clear of the desk, and opened my arms.

I encased her skinniness in my impressive arms and a faintly incestuous urge glimmered briefly and was drowned in my more familiar emotions.

She pulled away finally and turned to the man who had followed her in. "Didn't I tell you he was handsome, Homer?"

The man called Homer was about my size, range-tanned and Texas-tailored, a genial white-haired man. He nodded smilingly.

"You also said I didn't have a smidgen of business sense," I said to Aunt Sheila. "Because I heard it and so did everybody else on this floor." I came around to be introduced to her companion.

"You haven't," she said. "Jan has—but you—ugh!" She took a breath. "This is Homer Gallup, Brock. We were married in Las Vegas, Thursday."

I shook their hands, at a loss for words. I kissed Aunt Sheila once more. Then she stood more erectly and patted her flat tummy. "How about *that?*"

"Some girdle," I commented.

"Girdle, hell!" she said. "That's *belly,* boy, as we say in the Panhandle. Right, Homer?"

My aunt has a great gift of acclimation, a cunning, chameleon ability to be one thing to each one, the thing he wants most. With most men, that's easy.

Homer nodded in agreement, a little abashed at the terminology.

Aunt Sheila gushed on. "That's what two years in La Jolla can do for you—starve you. Best damned town in the world for starving."

"Auntie," I said patiently, "you were *never* fat."

"No, but I had some sag. Look at me now—thirty-seven years old and I wear a size ten."

"Shoe?" I asked.

Homer laughed.

And stopped laughing. Aunt Sheila does have rather large feet. Fashionably and aristocratically narrow—but long. She stared at Homer.

He gulped.

She said sweetly, "Tell Brock the remark you made about my feet last night, Homer."

"Naw," he said. "Let's forget it."

She turned to me. "He told me my feet were just right for stamping out grass fires."

I laughed.

I had laughed alone. In the uncomfortable silence, I asked, "Staying in town long?"

"We planned to," my aunt said. "We thought we'd like Beverly Hills—until we drove into this smog this morning."

"We thought we'd buy a place," Homer contributed, "and that girl friend of yours could help us pick furniture and we'd kind of get the feel of the town."

"Well," I said. "Well, well, well—"

My aunt looked at me suspiciously. "You don't want me around, do you? One of my few living relatives and you don't want me around."

"I love you," I said. "I want you around. Look, it's almost lunchtime—why don't I phone Jan and we can have lunch together?"

That started our afternoon. Jan said "Eeeee—yippee!" when I told her Aunt Sheila was in town. We arranged to meet her at Cini's.

There we floated a full Italian lunch on a sea of Martinis (for the girls), whiskey (for Homer) and two sedate beers for yours truly.

Jan and my aunt chatted as they always did when together, Homer chuckled genially and I watched Jan carefully.

She is an interior decorator, my Jan, and like my apparently giddy Aunt Sheila, she has a solid and active concern for the profit potential.

Don't get me wrong; I don't consider it a flaw. It is a sense I lack, this instinct for the maximum dollar, but I don't consider myself nobler because of it. Like the rest of us, Jan has to eat.

Aunt Sheila had already told her that Jan "of course" would decorate any house the newlyweds bought. Okay, there was my darling's profit—promised. For me, that would be enough.

But then they got to talking about houses and Jan said quite firmly, "There's only one realtor in Beverly Hills who really knows the area."

I smiled. Jan caught the smile but didn't blush. She looked at Homer levelly, all business, and went on. "I'll call him as soon as we're through eating and he can pick us up here."

Split commission, I thought. Jan doesn't advertise it, but she also holds a real estate broker's license. She would make a mint on the kind of decorating Aunt Sheila would order with that Texas money behind her. Was that enough for my Jan? No. There was a realtor's commission waiting to be split.

I said calmly, "Why don't we look around for a house

that isn't listed? Why pay a five per cent bonus to some realtor?''

Aunt Sheila shook her head. "It never works. I tried that in La Jolla. It's always better, all around, to go through a broker."

Jan said sweetly and patronizingly, "You mustn't listen to Brock, Homer. Brock is hopelessly naive when it comes to business."

Homer smiled in his genial way and said, "I'm like Brock. Business bores me. But I should think a girl in your profession would hold a real estate broker's license. They aren't hard to get."

A silence. Sheila was eating, Jan was staring at Homer doubtfully, Homer was grinning—and I was gloating.

Jan looked at me and back at Homer. Sheila asked, "Why the sudden silence? What's happened? Homer, did you say something rude again?"

He shook his head, smiling.

I said, "Homer has just given Jan some sound advice and she's digesting it."

Aunt Sheila's voice was ice. "I want to know what's going on. Homer, I want to know *right now!*

Jan's chin lifted, but she said nothing.

Homer appealed to me. "Did I say something wrong?"

"Nope."

Jan took a deep breath. "But I did, I guess." She looked at Sheila. "I was—crowding him. I'm ashamed of myself."

For a moment, the formerly festive spirit was dampened.

And then Homer said, "Nothing of the sort. You call that house-peddler friend of yours and have him here when we're finished eating." He grinned all around. "C'mon, one more drink won't hurt us." He winked at me. "And I don't mean beer."

Well, the hard stuff is not usually for me, but there was still a trace of coolness in the air and I owed it to Jan to help dispel what I could of that.

So I ordered a double bourbon and raised my voice a little. By the time Jan's broker friend arrived, we were almost back to our pre-lunch abandon.

His name was Wallace Darrow, a rather handsome gent around forty, smooth and genial. He insisted on buying another round of drinks before we left. It was almost three o'clock before we floated out to find the newlyweds a home.

It was a montage to me from there on, a confused memory of glass and redwood, Lannon stone and glass, fieldstone and redwood and glass, but always glass, glass, glass . . . .

Until Homer complained. "We're not goldfish, Mr. Darrow."

Darrow sighed. "You're not going to get away from a lot of glass, not in the new homes, Mr. Gallup."

"So show us some older homes then," Homer ordered.

Jan flinched and Aunt Sheila frowned. Wallace Darrow looked thoughtful, waiting for one of the girls to protest.

Aunt Sheila was now looking speculative. Aunt Sheila, experienced in male attitudes and mores, was holding back her protest. My Jan, however, was looking sly.

She smiled and said to winsome Wallace Darrow, "How about the Mary Mae Milgrim place, Wally?"

"Mary Mae Milgrim—?" Homer asked in awed wonder. "Is *her* house for sale?"

Darrow nodded and his glance matched my aunt's speculative look.

I said, "It's probably been for sale for thirty years, huh, Wallace?"

He looked at me coolly. "Not quite."

"Twenty-five?" I suggested. "When was her last picture?"

Wallace pretended he hadn't heard. Homer said nostalgically, "Mary Mae Milgrim—there'll never be another like her. I saw every picture she was ever in.''

Jan said, ''You could phone her, Wally, to find out if it's possible to see the house today.''

He nodded and smiled knowingly at Jan as Homer went over to inspect the view from the home we were standing in.

Sheila said softly, ''What's going on?''

Jan said, ''Once he sees this monstrosity, he'll stop talking about 'older homes.' It's the most grotesque thing south of San Simeon.''

''Girls,'' I warned them quietly, ''no shenanigans. I don't want any manipulation of my old buddy Homer Gallup.''

My Aunt Sheila said coolly, ''We intend to protect him from himself. Stay out of this, Rockhead.''

Homer turned from looking out the huge window and surveyed us all. ''Where'd that peddler go?''

Jan said, ''He went to phone Mary Mae Milgrim.''

''Great,'' Homer said. He looked around the immense living room we were standing in. ''What's a lean-to like this go for?''

''It's listed at a hundred and ten thousand,'' Jan said, ''but I'm sure it's open to an offer.''

Homer laughed. ''I'll bet it is. Cripes, he can't have more than two and a half acres here, and most of that hillside.'' He shook his head sadly.

Jan and Aunt Sheila exchanged scheming feminine glances and said nothing.

Then Darrow came back, all smiles, and said Miss Mary Mae Milgrim would be delighted to show us her house.

After all the yacking of the afternoon, this trip was comparatively quiet. Aunt Sheila and Jan were undoubtedly smirking inwardly, Homer looked adolescently expectant, and only another realtor would be able to guess what Darrow was thinking about.

Off one of Sunset's big turns, a pair of stone pillars

flanked a driveway that led up towards the hills. We turned
in and wound along a gravel driveway bordered by Lombardy poplars.

And then, suddenly ahead, the Mary Mae Milgrim mansion was in sight. I'll tell you no lie—it had *pennants* flying
from its turrets. It had all the "B's": Battlements and bal-
conies with balustrades. On the faded pennants, the proud
"M" for Mary Mae Milgrim was still faintly visible.

Jan looked at Aunt Sheila and Aunt Sheila looked sick.
Wallace Darrow looked smug—and Homer looked at me.

"Well, Brock—?" he said.

"Terrific," I said. "Magnificent. Worthy of the name
of Milgrim."

"Ye gods," Aunt Sheila whispered hoarsely. "It even
has a *moat!*"

The moat was dry and the chains connected to the timbered
bridge were rusty, if immense.

"I wonder if the bridge lifts?" Homer said wonderingly.

Darrow coughed discreetly. "I—uh—believe it's inopera-
tive at the moment. But I'm sure it can be repaired."

Jan looked at Darrow suspiciously. She and Aunt Sheila
were losing an ally. For Mr. Wallace Darrow was not in
the business to sell the customer what *he* liked, but only
what the customer would like—and *buy*. A sale is a sale is
a sale, and when you sell a white elephant, it's a supersale.

I chuckled.

Aunt Sheila asked, "What's so damned funny, Tasteless?
I always knew you favored your father's side of the family."

Aunt Sheila was my mother's brother's wife. He had died
young and released her for greener pastures. I said nothing.

Homer said, "Look at that construction. Solid stone. By
golly, this place isn't all glass."

"There is some glass, Homer," Jan said meekly. "There
are a lot of windows and some of them are almost eighteen
inches wide."

Homer laughed. "Oh, you young ones—Glass, glass, glass. All glass is good for is wrapping whiskey in."

And we laughed, Homer and I, as the car stopped in the courtyard, in the *cobbled* courtyard, and we got out.

"Authentic," Homer said. "Authentic as hell, by golly."

"Authentic Chas Addams," Jan agreed. "Where would a decorator start, with a place like this?"

"You'd have to start with dynamite and a bulldozer," my Aunt Sheila said. "Level it, I say."

Homer stiffened and swiveled slowly to stare at his bride. She lifted her chin and returned the stare.

Homer asked politely, softly, "Don't you even want to see the inside?"

A pause, and then she said quietly, "If you do, I do."

Nobody had any further comments to offer as we walked along toward the high, broad, brass-studded front door.

The door opened before we had a chance to ring the bell and a woman stood there, waiting for us to identify ourselves.

It wasn't Mary Mae. This girl was around thirty, black-haired, blue-eyed, slim and serene.

Wallace said, "I phoned Miss Milgrim about fifteen minutes ago. I'm Wallace Darrow."

"Come in," the girl said. "I'm Joyce Thorne, Miss Milgrim's secretary."

We came into a lofty, musty entry hall, complete with lances, tapestries and an enormous medallion set into one wall, a huge scarlet-enameled "M" set into a background of peeling gilt. The alliteration of Mary Mae Milgrim was apparently symbolic to her.

"Authentic," Homer said again in admiration.

"Genuine early Pathé," Jan admitted. "A grand house for orgies."

Homer looked at her skeptically and then Miss Thorne said, "This way, please."

We went through a high, narrow archway into a room two stories high, with a beamed ceiling. It was dim in here, damp and cool. A fireplace big enough to roast an elephant divided the long wall, and the furniture was solid oak early mission. The drapes over the narrow windows were maroon velvet and they were closed this smoggy April day. Consequently, the room was dark enough so that the illusion at the far end of the room was adequate for devoted Mary Mae Milgrim fans.

For the lady stood there, slim and proud in black velvet, not a wrinkle visible from this distance, the creamy white skin flawless in the shadowed room. One hand rested lightly on the back of a refectory chair as she smiled at us graciously.

"Good afternoon, guests," she said melodiously. "Which one is Mr. Wallace?"

"Mr. Darrow," Wallace corrected her. "Wallace Darrow, Miss Milgrim, of Darrow, Weldon and Lutz." And then he introduced us.

When it was Homer's turn, he bowed with true Texas courtliness, and said warmly, "I consider this, Miss Milgrim, the high point of my life. You will always be the greatest of them all to me."

There was a momentary silence after that tribute.

And then Miss Milgrim nodded acknowledgment to Homer and said to Darrow, "I'm not sure if you're familiar with the house. Miss Thorne will be your guide."

This much I'll say for the place: it had a lot of rooms. The servants' rooms were small and the other rooms were large, but all of them had narrow windows and high ceilings.

Both Homer and Jan were shaking their heads as we went from room to room, but I am sure their thoughts were not the same.

Eventually we came back to the big, dim room where Miss Milgrim waited. Homer, I could see, was ripe for the harpoon, and it seemed certain that Darrow would know it if I did. Jan seemed resigned, though she is unpredictable. My Aunt Sheila was looking thoughtful, glancing at Homer constantly, as though appraising him.

Miss Milgrim was sitting in the refectory chair, back straight, chin well lifted, in an admirable attempt at gracious poise. There weren't many people who would be anxious to buy this mausoleum; she couldn't afford to look too hungry.

Homer said, "It's a wonderful house, Miss Milgrim. In perfect taste."

Jan blanched. Aunt Sheila kept her face carefully blank. Darrow glanced between Homer and Miss Milgrim and there were dollar signs in his eyes.

Miss Milgrim said, "Thank you, Mr. Gallup. I doubt if you'll find many houses as soundly constructed in *this* town."

There was some scorn in her voice. *This* was the town that had forgotten Mary Mae Milgrim.

The ringmaster, Darrow, looked around at all of us and came up with the cliché I was waiting for. He said earnestly, "They just don't build them like this any more."

Next to me, Jan whispered, "Thank God!"

Miss Milgrim said, "I'm sure you'll want to talk with your clients in private. I'll expect to hear from you, Mr. Darrow."

That was our dismissal. Homer once again told Miss Milgrim what a wonderful house she had and the five of us went out to Darrow's car.

There, Homer asked, "How much?"

"It's listed at a hundred and forty thousand," Darrow said. "The land alone should be worth that."

Homer looked at his bride, "Well, Sheila—?"

Aunt Sheila hesitated, looking at Jan. Jan made no comment. Aunt Sheila said softly, "You love the place, don't you, Homer?"

He nodded, and his face was a little boy's. "I guess it's kind of old-fashioned, huh? But Jan could fix that up, couldn't she?"

Jan looked at the cobblestones in the courtyard and didn't answer. Aunt Sheila said, "If anyone could, Jan could. Homer, it's your money and I'm happy any place where you're happy."

Darrow was busily leafing through his book, getting the details on the house. He said, "A hundred and forty thousand is the *asking* price, Mr. Gallup. I'm sure it's open to an offer."

Homer shook his head. "If Miss Milgrim wants a hundred and forty thousand, that's what she'll get. We don't chisel Miss Mary Mae Milgrim, not on any deal where *I'm* involved."

Darrow shrugged and continued to look through the listing. Then he said, "There's a rather strange condition to any sale, I see." He frowned. "Perhaps Miss Milgrim would be willing to waive it."

"What is it?" Aunt Sheila asked hopefully.

"There's a servants' cottage over at the north end of the property," Darrow explained, "of three bedrooms and a bath and a half. Miss Milgrim wants to retain the right to live in it, rent free, for the rest of her life."

Sheila frowned, waiting a reaction from Homer. Jan looked hopeful.

But Homer took a deep breath and studied his future home with the look of a lad viewing his first Christmas tree. "Wonderful," he said rapturously. "All this—and Mary Mae Milgrim too!"

TWO

DARROW HAD ALL the forms with him; he suggested he take Homer's offer, accompanied by check, right back into the house.

Jan looked at him levelly and said, "What's the hurry, Wallace? It's been on the market a long time."

Wallace said nothing for seconds, thinking his realtor's thoughts. It was through Jan that Wallace had met Homer Gallup; how close the association was he didn't know at the moment.

They stared at each other—and Homer said, "That's right, Mr. Darrow, there's no hurry." He looked at this bride. "You're not crazy for the house are you?"

A veteran of three marriages, a woman who had given her life to pleasing men, my aunt smiled and said, "If you are, Homer, I am." She glanced at the diamond-circled wrist watch he had given her on their wedding day. "But it's late, and I'm getting hungry. The house will still be here tomorrow."

Homer turned around to survey it hungrily once more. Darrow said, "I'll run back in, then, and tell Miss Milgrim we're leaving."

In my naïve way, I thought we had already left. I was glad I had never gone into real estate; it's a very complicated business.

He went back to the house, and we climbed into his car. Jan sat next to me and stared moodily out the window. My girl is in business and *any* business can occasionally make you squirm guiltily. Unfortunately, my girl also sells taste and when her need for a buck conflicts with that, she's in serious ethical trouble.

From the front seat, Aunt Sheila turned around to ask, "Why so quiet, baby?"

Jan looked at the back of Homer's neck and took a breath. Finally, she said quietly, "I've been a *schtunk,* a real *schtunk.*"

In the rear-view mirror, I could see Homer's smile. He didn't turn around.

Jan said, "Homer, I do have a real estate broker's license. And I was going to split the commission with Wallace Darrow."

Homer, that gallant, turned around and smiled at my love. "Why not? Why should Darrow get it all?"

"I refuse to take it now," she went on grimly. "I'll take my split from Wally and refund it to you."

He chuckled. "You won't do anything of the kind. Now, you sit back and think of a good place to have dinner and forget all about that piddling little commission." He winked at me. "You've got a real little live wire there, Brock."

"And with a conscience," I said. "Every day, she surprises me."

She surprised me again. I'd expected a dig in the ribs for that remark. But she only snuggled closer and continued to stare gloomily out at the door through which Darrow had disappeared.

My sweet Aunt Sheila said, "Outside of Brock (Rockhead) Callahan, who is completely honest? And what has it got *him?*"

"Inner peace," I told her loftily. "What in the hell is that five percenter doing in there, trying to make time with Miss Thorne?"

The door opened then, and Darrow appeared. Over his shoulder, I could see the serene face of Joyce Thorne, Miss Milgrim's secretary. They seemed to be having a lot to say to each other.

Shenanigans . . . ?

Homer said, "That Miss Thorne is a pretty little thing, isn't she?"

"And how," I said.

The girls didn't comment.

Then Wallace finished whatever hanky-panky he had been arranging and came down our way. He slid in behind the wheel and sighed. Before he started the engine, he took another admiring look at the house and said sadly, "They just don't build them like that any more."

"Maybe there's no market for them any more." I said, and watched his face in the mirror.

Nothing showed on the face. He swung the car around and went heading out over the drawbridge and back toward the world of today.

The car was heavy with silence. The alliance of the girls and Wallace against the Gallup-Callahan axis had been disturbed. We were all individuals again, with our individual peeves and urges. Wallace could undoubtedly sense this and his two and a half per cent of a hundred and forty thousand dollars was riding the edge of calamity.

He must have realized that too much silence could solidify alien attitudes, so he broke it as we turned onto Sunset: "If you're looking for an older home, Mr. Gallup, the thing you have to remember is that mostly they're in run-down neighborhoods. Luckily, here in Beverly Hills, we realtors have managed to resist the invasion of that kind of blight. Living there, in that ancestral masterpiece, your investment would be vigilantly protected."

Not a nickel had changed hands, but he already had Homer living in the joint. I stared out the car window at the singing traffic streaming around the long curves and kept my peace.

So did Homer, though he nodded.

"California," Wallace went on, "like the great sovereign state of Texas, is an expanding, and *exploding* economy. Secluded havens like the Milgrim mansion get rarer and rarer. In all my thousands of listings, I doubt if I have more than half a dozen places like that."

This time Homer didn't nod.

Don't crowd him, Wallace, I thought. *Don't fence him in. There is a time to talk and a time to shut up. Don't overplay your strong hand. Be wary, Wallace.*

Wallace Darrow, of Darrow, Weldon and Lutz could have been psychic, for he suddenly shut up. We drove in heavenly silence for blocks.

Back at Cini's, where he had picked us up, he dropped us off. He glanced at Jan and said to Homer, "Shall I phone you in the morning, then, sir? Or wait to hear from you?"

Homer said, "I'm not sure where I'll be. I'd better phone you."

A pause, while Darrow studied him thoughtfully. Then Homer climbed heavily from the car and we all got out. A general air of depression seemed to hang over us.

Darrow forced a smile and said, "In the morning, then." His big car glided mournfully away.

Aunt Sheila looked at Cini's and said, "We're not going to eat here again, are we?"

"It's not food I need," Homer said glumly. "It's liquor and sweet music, to drown out the memory of Wallace Darrow's voice." He put a hand on my shoulder. "Brock, am I sensitive, or did that walking mouth get to you, too?"

"Almost," I said. "Getting adjusted to a California realtor, Homer, is almost as bad as getting adjusted to a first marriage. I wish I was a drinking man, so I could join you."

"You're a drinking man tonight," Homer said, squeezing my shoulder. "Please? For me?"

Well, for Homer . . . . For Aunt Sheila's finest recent

husband . . . . And Jan would be making money off him . . . .

"I'm with you," I said.

We started at Romanoff's and wound up at the Palladium and that is quite a gap, as any local will tell you. We ate and danced and drank. And because I rarely touch the hard stuff, it got to me, making the last few hours of our evening a semi-blank!

I wakened in the morning with no memory of how I got home. My back ached and my legs were weak and my mouth tasted like a full ash tray, though I hadn't done any smoking. The bad legs and back could be attributed to my dancing, another of my rare vices.

Over my black, black coffee, I tried to recall the highlights of my festive evening, but they were dim. I remember dancing with Jan and Aunt Sheila at the Palladium; I remember a beatnik coffeehouse and a first-rate guitarist.

My phone rang. The pleasant voice identified its owner as Joyce Thorne, Miss Milgrim's secretary. Miss Milgrim, according to Miss Thorne, had been trying to reach Mr. Darrow and having no luck.

"It's probably too early for him to be at the office," I told her. "I don't know the man, but Miss Bonnet might have his home number."

There was a long pause. And then Miss Thorne said, "I—haven't been completely truthful, Mr. Callahan. To be frank with you, Miss Milgrim was wondering about Mr. Gallup's interest in the house, and she hasn't his number—and—well, she didn't want to phone Mr. Darrow."

"And you called me," I finished for her. "How did you remember my name?"

"Everyone is familiar with your name, Mr. Callahan, a famous athlete like you."

Pure hogwash, of course, but phrased so sweetly and spoken so melodiously that my heart went out to the dear, loyal girl.

I asked gently, "Is it very important to Miss Milgrim to sell that house?"

Another long pause. Then: "It isn't something I'd admit to Mr. Darrow or want you to repeat to him, but it is. She needs the money desperately."

"And you were afraid Mr. Darrow might guess that and suggest a lower offer to Mr. Gallup?"

"Well—yes—something like that." A sniff. "Oh, I'm so embarrased— This sounds so—*dumb.*"

"It's not dumb at all," I assured her. "It's sweet and loyal. Just between us, Mr. Darrow did suggest a lower offer and Mr. Gallup would have none of it. He said he would never chisel on the sublime Mary Mae Milgrim. And he does like the house—that much I can tell you. I'm sure you'll hear from him."

She thanked me fervently and hung up.

It was possible that Miss Milgrim had asked her to call me. But thinking back to her conversation in the doorway with Darrow yesterday, it was also possible that Darrow had asked her to call. Darrow could guess by now that sentiment was a bigger element than greed in the make-up of Homer Gallup. And this oblique approach could be a clincher.

I decided not to tell Homer that she had called.

My morning was occupied with an investigation, a discreet check for a wealthy client whose daughter was enamored of an engaging but apparently poor young man. The investigation carried over into the afternoon and revealed the young man as a fortune hunter and embryonic con man.

I made my report in person and sat down to a mid-afternoon lunch at the drugstore, weary in body and sad in spirit. My frequent role as the murderer of Cupid always depresses me.

My fan behind the counter said, "Brock, old buddy, what'll it be?"

"Hemlock," I said. "Unless you can suggest something better."

He looked at me compassionately. "Blue? Wish you were back with the Rams?"

I shook my head. "I'm too old and too slow and too cowardly. I just wish I lived in a better world."

He nodded in empathic agreement. And then said softly, "The spare ribs are pretty good for drugstore spare ribs. Country style."

Food helps. It's always a help with me. The ribs were good and so were the browned potatoes and my fan made a fresh carafe of coffee while I was eating.

I was on my second cup of that when someone took the stool next to mine. I turned to gaze at my love.

"Hello," she said dully. And to my fan, "Coffee, please. And are there any fresh sweet rolls?"

"Bear claws," he said. "I'll warm one."

Jan sighed.

I said, "You look despondent. What happened?"

"Homer bought — that monstrosity."

"And you made two and a half per cent of a hundred and forty thousand dollars," I said. I wrinkled my forehead. "That comes to a quick thirty-five-hundred-dollar commission for scheming little Jan Bonnet. And money is your god. So, I repeat, why are you despondent?"

"Shut up," she said. "You don't have to say money is my god. Taste—that's my god, good taste."

I smiled, saying nothing.

"Just because you're an economic idiot," she went on, "you assume the reasonable business or professional person worships money. Do you think you're the only professional man in the world with ethical standards?"

"No'm. I'm one of the few I've met, though."

"Huh!" she said. "You—you—egocentric—slob!"

I sipped my coffee.

"You muscle," she went on. "You outsized Puck."

"You're projecting," I soothed her. "You're hating yourself and taking it out on me. What is *really* bugging you, little one?"

Her coffee was in front of her now. She sipped it and sniffed.

"This is old Brock the Rock," I said quietly. "This is your last, best hope. Confide in me, tempestuous one."

"Damn you," she said. "Smart aleck. My hope? My blind alley, that's you. My nothing man leading me nowhere."

"Easy," I said. "Don't go too far. Even with me, there are limits, Jan Bonnet. Now, calm down or shut up."

She turned to glare at me and I looked away. My fan came over and put the warm bear claw, loaded with sliced almonds, in front of her.

"Special for you, Miss Bonnet, with an extra pat of butter."

She looked at the bear claw and up at the counterman and her chin began to quiver.

He smiled at her. "Brock's right—this time. You were unreasonable."

"Men—" she said.

He winked at me and went to serve someone at the other end of the counter. Nothing from Jan and only a waiting, smiling patience from me.

Until finally she said, "He wants me to decorate that place. Homer, I mean. He wants me to decorate it *in keeping with the architecture*. That was his phrase."

"You'll make a mint on it,' I said.

"Right! And if money was my god, would I be unhappy about a job that big?"

I shrugged. "If money wasn't important to you, you'd simply tell him you're too busy right now."

She said evenly, "I never said money wasn't important

to me. I never heard any *sane* person say that. You're always twisting things I say."

"Honey," I said calmly, "why fight it? You're going to take the job. If you need an opiate for your artistic conscience, think of the job as a *challenge*. Because it will certainly be that. It won't be a triumph, but it sure as hell is a challenge, right?"

She looked at me suspiciously.

"One of us has to be sensible," I said. "We'll never get married on my income."

She sniffed again. "You and your ethics! But you'd live on a woman's income, wouldn't you?"

I shook my head solemnly. "Not on *any* woman's. I'd have to love her. That, beloved hothead, is ethics."

She sipped her coffee. "A challenge," she said, mostly to herself.

I had given her a rationalization and she was mulling it. My fan came over to pour her fresh coffee.

"A challenge—" she said, more softly this time, and there was a glint in her eyes.

"Did Mary Mae get her gardener's cottage, like she wanted?" I asked.

Jan nodded. "And that so-called secretary of hers is moving right in with her. Wally thinks that Joyce Thorne is special. Do you think she's so special?"

I said diplomatically, "I didn't get a good look at her. Did Darrow, Weldon and Lutz, by any chance, have an exclusive on that house?"

Jan looked at me sharply. "Yes. Why? I was the one who suggested we look at it."

"That's right. I forgot. What's the mortgage?"

Jan shook her head. "No mortgage. It's probably the only unmortgaged place in Beverly Hills."

"Come on," I said. "The word I got is that Miss Milgrim was in desperate need of money."

Jan stared at me. "Mary Mae Milgrim? Are you crazy? Ye gods, she owns two office buildings on the Strip, an apartment house in Westwood, and a whole damned business block in the Palisades. Penurious, yes, but in need of money—? Like Rockfeller."

"I've been conned," I said quietly. "That—witch." I took a breath and told Jan about Joyce Thorne's morning phone call.

"She called you? And where did she get your number?"

"In the phone book. Where else?"

"And how come she remembered your name?"

My fan had overheard that question, and he answered for me. "Brock (the Rock) Callahan, Miss Bonnet? You're not serious, are you? The greatest guard who ever played football? You can't be serious."

I tried to look modest, a major effort.

Jan waved at my fan for silence and continued with her interrogation of me. "There isn't a—a *decent* reason I can think of why she should phone you. You weren't in any way involved in the sale of that property."

"I don't know why she called me," I said levelly, "and stop thinking of the indecent reason why she might have. My own personal hunch is Wallace Darrow of Darrow, Weldon and Lutz had his fine hand in it somehow, but that's just a hunch. I was the only famous person at the house yesterday and it's logical I could be the only name she remembered. She said she didn't want to call Darrow, because she thought he might guess they were too hungry for the sale and suggest a lower offer to Homer."

The counterman nodded, silently supporting my thoughtful explanation. This was one man who had never deserted me.

Jan looked at him and at me, shook her head, and finished her bear claw. She wiped her mouth daintily with a paper napkin and said, "Why do you hate Wally Darrow so much? Because he's successful?"

"I swear to you I didn't even know he was successful. He struck me as a rather tricky eager beaver, which annoyed me, but I don't hate him. Or anybody else—at the moment."

Jan took out a cigarette and my fan held a light for her. Then he left us and my girl stared moodily straight ahead.

"Anything else new?" I asked her.

She sighed. "A party. Homer wants a big party in that— that mausoleum before I start the decorating."

"What will he use for furniture? He didn't buy Mary Mae's furniture, did he?"

"No. She's leaving a few pieces there, enough for the kind of party Homer wants. He doesn't know many people in town, so he suggested I invite my friends. And maybe some of yours. He wants a lot of young people around, he says."

I chuckled.

"What's funny?" she asked.

"I was thinking of your—colleagues," I explained, "the male members of your profession. I was thinking Homer would be surprised to see a party where boys brought boys. It might confuse him."

Jan said coolly. "I planned to invite some of my *female* friends, for your information, Mr. Callahan."

"Great!" I said. "And I'll invite some Rams."

"Some ex-Rams, you mean? The poker players?"

"Fine fellows, all of them. First class party boys. Old Homer's kind of people, authentic."

She studied me thoughtfully. And then, wonder of wonders, she smiled! "Brock," she said, "we need a party, don't we?"

I nodded.

"Invite more of those slim halfbacks," she said, "and fewer of those overweight guards, won't you?"

THREE

IT WAS A heterogeneous group, as the professors say. Because not only did Jan invite her friends, there were also mine and a few of Aunt Sheila's, one of Homer's—and a host of Mary Mae Milgrim's.

These gentle, faded flowers from a better, lost world were like half-remembered dreams, faces that had once stirred the multitudes but were unidentifiable today.

Unidentifiable to most, but not to Homer, that ancient cinema fan. He was enchanted, he was in the shadowland of his youth.

He clapped me on the shoulder and waved expansively. "Look at me," he said, "little old Homer Gallup from Gila Creek, surrounded by the greatest names in show business."

I looked around and nodded agreement, sharing his moment.

"And from the sports world," he added generously, "immortals, all."

I smiled modestly.

In one corner, half-screened by a potted palm, Wallace Darrow and Joyce Thorne were laughing gaily together. I said, "All this, and Wallace Darrow too. Homer, you're a tolerant man."

He shrugged. "Can I hate the man who found me this wonderful place?"

"It was Jan who suggested it," I reminded him.

Homer frowned and then nodded thoughtfully. "By golly, it was! I'd forgotten that. She suggested it to Darrow, didn't she?"

Jan nodded.

Homer smiled at her and winked at me. "And now I have a feeling she doesn't even want to decorate the place."

"I want to," Jan said, and glanced at me. "I consider it a *challenge,* Homer." She met his gaze, her chin high.

In the ballroom, the musicians had started and I took my semi-honest girl friend by the hand and led her that way.

"Money," she murmured, "money, money, money, money—"

"It makes the wheels turn," I consoled her. "It affords employment and supports the scholarships. Don't brood; it's a party night."

"Damn you, Brock Callahan," she said. "Why does it have to be *you?*"

I didn't answer. I took her into my arms and moved with guardlike grace onto the immense and glistening floor. Some of my contemporaries were there, dancing with their wives. And some of my wifeless contemporaries stood alongside the floor, waiting for the proper shapes to appear.

"Rams," Jan said. "The joint is jumping with ex-Rams and former cinema stars. The place is haunted with yesterday's heroes."

"The music is soft and the booze expensive," I whispered in her perfumed ear. "Relax, Jan Bonnet. It's a night for romance."

"Romance—" she said. "To you, that just means *sex!*"

"To me, too," a voice said. "How about cutting in?"

It was Scooter Calvin, a former Ram, a hundred and eighty pounds of scat-back, handsome, rich and single.

Jan blushed and I said, "Later, Scooter. Not right now. This is our first dance and we're in love."

He shook his head. "A girl like that—with a lousy guard." He went away.

In my arms, the fine body of Jan Bonnet was tense and rebellious. She is a fairly complex girl, loving both beauty and money, and it is not easy for her to adjust to our present civilization. She is a girl of many moods, but I love her in all of them. She is the beginning and the end. She is Jan; what can I say?

Some of her tenseness left and she moved closer to me. "Do you realize," she asked quietly, "that this makes two times this week we've danced together?"

"We're young," I explained, "and courting. After we're married, I'll put an end to this nonsense."

After we're married. . . . We'd never be married. She didn't like my job and she couldn't live on the salary a high school coaching job might bring me. And what else could I do?

An aged couple swept past us, the man in antiquated tails, the lady in faded black velvet. Their heads were high, their steps firm.

"Do you think they're still courting?" Jan asked.

"It's possible," I said, "that they've both been married a dozen times and are again courting. This is a romantic town, in some ways."

I thought Jan shivered. I know she moved closer.

Beauty and money she loved. Kids and Cadillacs. Poor Jan.

She said, "This looks like one of the Arthur Murray shows on TV. You know, the gold medal winners—"

"You need a drink," I said.

"And how," she answered.

I only drank beer, myself, except on rare occasions. And only Einlicher, if I could get it. Homer, because of his great regard for me, had stocked all four of the temporary bars with Einlicher, the finest beer in the world.

While I drank the beer, Jan gulped a double Scotch. And then Randy Roman came over. In the old days, Randy had played tackle to my guard and was now a coach at a Valley high school.

He wanted to dance with Jan and I gave them my blessing. Randy was a pretty good dancer, for a tackle, and I watched them in admiration.

Then next to me, a thin and sallow man said, "Einlicher, eh? Mr. Gallup has a discerning taste."

"I told him about it," I said, and tried to remember where I had seen him before. "My name is Brock Callahan," I added.

"Of course," he said. "I have seen you with the Rams, many times. But you don't remember me, do you?"

I frowned. "Sort of—"

"Enrico Rivali," he said.

Now I knew him. He had been a writer-director here before Italians were in vogue, during the Hungarian regime. He had come to fame on the rise of Mary Mae Milgrim.

I said, "Of course. Miss Milgrim's favorite writer and director." I shook his thin, strong hand. "You're in television now, I suppose?"

He shook his head sadly. "I could never adjust to the medium. No scope, no time, no attention to the important detail, a frivolous and degraded art form."

"Have an Einlicher," I said, "and tell me about it."

He smiled bleakly. "What is there to tell? I was once important. I no longer am. I once functioned. I no longer do. This area has known a million stories with the same plot."

"Well, then," I said, "have an Einlicher and let's look at the girls. You may not be famous, but you're still a Latin."

His smile was less bleak. "Ah, yes—the girls. They have helped to make these recent years bearable. Except for them,

I'm sure I would have gone back to Italy, back to the farm.''

Scooter Calvin was dancing with Jan now. My eyes searched the crowd and I saw Horse Malone moving ponderously around the floor with Joyce Thorne in his arms.

"That Thorne girl's a stunner, isn't she?" I asked Enrico Rivali.

He shrugged. "I guess. She bothers me. I can't figure that girl."

"So—?"

"She gives the impression she is devoted to Mary Mae and working for almost nothing, but I happen to know she is very well paid."

"From Mary Mae you heard that?"

He raised his eyebrows. "Who else?"

I withheld comment. Mary Mae was the one I couldn't figure. I remembered what Jan had told me about the apartment house, the office buildings and the business property. I thought of the servants' cottage she had insisted on keeping, rent free. But Homer would be paying the taxes on it.

Enrico Rivali said thoughtfully, "I wonder if Mr. Gallup would be interested in financing a really artistic picture."

"Starring Miss Milgrim?" I asked.

He nodded, a speculative look in his eyes. "He admires Miss Milgrim, doesn't he?"

"Yup. But, Enrico—lay off Homer Gallup."

His sallow face stiffened and his dark eyes were hard as he stared at me. "Are you his manager?"

I shook my head. "I'm his friend. He's a sentimental man and I've appointed myself his guardian in this particular jungle."

Enrico smiled cynically. "Do you think he needs your advice? He's a millionaire. Are you?"

"Nope. I'm just Homer's friend. Now, you've been warned, Enrico. And the subject is closed."

He said something in Italian then, something pornographic, and walked abruptly away from me. I was sad; we'd started off so well.

I finished my beer and went over to cut in on Horse Malone, still dancing with Joyce Thorne.

I'm no Astaire, understand, but I'm pretty good at my own particular dance, which I refer to as the one-step-glide-and-hold. Joyce followed perfectly.

She looked up, after a few seconds, and said, "Savior."

"Was that Horse rough on you?"

"Maybe it was my fault. I was trying to dance to this orchestra and he was apparently listening to some other one I couldn't hear. What were you and Enrico talking about?"

"About girls. Why?"

"I wondered. He's a—a schemer. He'd still be pressing olives if it hadn't been for Miss Milgrim."

And what would you be doing? I thought, but didn't say.

"Weren't they married at one time?" I asked.

"Never!" she said sharply. "And their much publicized romance existed only in the publicist's idiotic mind."

"You don't like Enrico, I gather."

"I don't like any kind of parasite," she said.

Well, well. The pot and the kettle. Her body was slim and responsive, her perfume distracting, her grace reassuring. I tried an extra step without hesitation and she didn't falter. I added a tricky side step.

Over her head, I could see Jan dancing with Homer, and Jan's gaze was steady and suspicious. I waved.

"That's the girl you came with, isn't it?" Joyce asked. "Miss Bonnet, isn't it?"

"Right on both counts," I agreed, "but don't let it discourage you. She's broad-minded."

I was putting her through a rather intricate reverse turn when Meat Kowalski, another ex-guard, tapped my shoulder.

I relinquished her and went back to the bar.

Wallace was there, talking with Aunt Sheila. It didn't seem to be friendly, party talk, so I went into the living room, to another bar.

Again, a familiar face was here, a rather distinguished face, with a high forehead and an aquiline nose, a matinee idol face, now aged and gray.

He turned and smiled at me. "The great Brock Callahan, I believe?"

I had to come through and my memory didn't fail me. I smiled in return and said, "And the immortal John Davenport."

"My friends call me Jack," he said as we shook hands.

He had been one of the biggest names of the silent screen, sending the females into swoons from coast to coast and beyond these shores. He had been big, big, big. . . .

"Immortal—?" he said. "Not quite. Wouldn't 'lucky' be a better word?"

"It's luck that you're immortal, sure. Luck and talent did it. Are you retired now?" I ordered an Einlicher.

"Not quite," he said, and ordered a Scotch and water. "I've found a few bits here and there, since my agent deserted me." He lifted his glass. "Monstrous people, agents. Scrambling, absurd people."

"Even real estate agents," I agreed. "But I suppose God had some purpose in mind."

"Let's not be sentimental," he said, "about agents. This freak who represented me kept insisting I was too big. Too big for this bit and too big for that walk-on. In his cretin mind I was apparently too big for anything but starving. Finally, I was so big he dropped me."

"And your position improved?" I asked.

"Immeasurably. You see, I don't need much. I eat very little and drink only when someone else is pouring. But I must act. I either act or I die—it is that simple. I am a ham.

I come from a great sugar-cured tradition. Today, I am again alive.''

"You must have a lot of friends in the industry," I said. "You should do all right on your own."

"In this industry," he said firmly, "*nobody* has *any* friends."

"How about Mary Mae Milgrim?" I asked him. "She invited you to the party, didn't she?"

"To add tone," he explained, "and for some reason which I will probably learn later. You know, for years Mary Mae tried to get me for her leading man." He shrugged. "But—"

"You were too big," I guessed.

"I was too smart," he corrected me. "She dominated every picture she was ever in. Rivali saw to that, that— *schemer*."

I sipped my beer and thought about this and that. I asked, "When was the last time, before tonight, that you've seen or heard from Mary Mae Milgrim?"

"It's been years," he said. "This invitation was out of the blue. That's why I'm worried."

"But you came," I pointed out.

He lifted his glass. "I explained about that. I will eat well, drink only her best—and be prepared for any eventuality."

"It isn't her booze," I said. "It's Homer Gallup's. And I have a hunch Rivali thinks he can con Homer into producing another Mary Mae Milgrim picture." I lifted my glass. "With you in the secondary lead."

"I'm ready for it," he said. "I'm sure I can protect myself in the close-ups."

We drank solemnly, thinking our separate thoughts. Mine were defensive; I owed it to Homer to protect him from these hungry ghosts. In this motley group, there were undercurrents, Hollywood inspired.

Aunt Sheila came from the ballroom, her eyes stormy. She came to the bar and ordered a double bourbon. She drank it in three gulps, ignoring Mr. Davenport and me.

She ordered another, and I said, "Easy now. The night's young."

She turned to look at me. "You know what I learned today?"

"I'm all ears."

"I heard this house was in escrow six months, but something went wrong."

"So—?"

"It was in escrow at a purchase price of *eighty-five thousand dollars!*"

"And—?"

"And? We paid a hundred and forty thousand. That's a difference of fifty-five thousand dollars, idiot nephew."

"Don't call me names," I told her firmly. "I didn't sell it to you. And much as I hate to come to the defense of Wallace Darrow, he suggested that Homer offer a lower price. And Homer refused."

"But did Darrow tell us about that earlier escrow?"

"Not in my hearing."

"Do you think it would have been more ethical if he had?"

I gave it some thought. "It would depend, I suppose, on whether Wallace was representing you or Miss Milgrim."

"It would, would it? Who dreamed up that fine distinction?"

I didn't get a chance to answer. Homer appeared at my shoulder, and Homer said soothingly, "Now, Sheila, don't spoil the party." He smiled at John Davenport. "Right, Mr. Davenport?"

"My friends call me Jack," Davenport said. "It's a fine party, Mr. Gallup."

"My friends call me Homer," our host said. "By gad, I think I saw every picture you were ever in."

"Pure masochism," Davenport commented. "Have you had the pleasure of speaking with Enrico Rivali this evening?"

Homer nodded. "And with Miss Milgrim. They tell me you're available for the picture they're planning."

"It's possible," Davenport said. "Did they tell you where they hoped to get the money for the picture?"

Homer frowned, looked uncomfortably at his bride, and said nothing.

Aunt Sheila's eyes widened and her head went back. "Homer—!"

"Now, Sheila, I didn't promise anything. It was just—talk."

My aunt finished her second double bourbon and looked around at all of us as though we were Forty-niner fans. Then she announced, "I'm going to have a little talk with Miss Mary Mae Milgrim!"

"Sheila, please—" Homer protested.

But she walked off stiffly and Homer didn't follow. He ordered bourbon and water and stared after her gloomily.

Then he sighed and turned to me. "Do you understand 'em?"

"Women?' I shook my head. "Maybe that's their attraction. Of course, Aunt Sheila's a little drunk right now. She has a better side, you know, Homer."

He raised a hand. "Don't get me wrong. I love her very much. But she's sure been ornery since she found out about the house. And what the hell difference does it make? It's only money."

My kind of man, Homer Gallup. I was proud to have him in the family.

Then Jan came looking for me and looked relieved when she saw I wasn't with Joyce Thorne. Where, she wanted to know, was Sheila?

"Looking for Mary Mae," I told her.

"I wonder where she's gone," Jan said. "Wallace Darrow was looking for her, too."

At the bar, John Davenport put down his drink and stared thoughtfully at all of us. "Missing? Mary Mae? It isn't at all like her to leave a party early."

"So maybe she's in the powder room," Homer said.

"Wallace has been looking for twenty minutes," Jan said. "She wouldn't need that much powder."

"Maybe she's out in the courtyard, necking," I suggested. "There's a full moon, you know." I looked at Davenport. "Is there any reason why we should be worried?"

He said slowly, "Possibly not. However, there are a number of people here who have reason to hate Miss Milgrim. People she invited to this party." He looked at Homer. "I know that seems unusual to a straightforward man, Mr. Gallup, but friends who hate you are a part of the local pattern."

Homer frowned and looked at me. I continued to give my attention to John Davenport. "You're not suggesting any of the guests would hate Miss Milgrim enough to—to do her bodily harm?"

Davenport shrugged. "She's missing, isn't she?"

"She's not in sight from where we stand," I agreed. "But that doesn't mean she's missing. This is a big house."

Homer said, "Maybe we'd better—" and that was as far as the sentence went.

Because from outside the house somewhere, we heard a horrible scream, and though I didn't recognize the voice, Homer did, immediately.

"My God," he said, "that's Sheila. Let's go."

He and I went out the French doors right next to the bar and heard Aunt Sheila scream again. To our left, we saw a flashlight; we ran that way, toward the drawbridge.

"We're coming!" Homer called. "Hang on, Sheila."

We were closer now and we could see that Aunt Sheila was not alone. A young Japanese boy, one of Miss Milgrim's servants hired for the night, was with her. He had the flashlight.

As we approached, we could see that he and Aunt Sheila were standing on the edge of the moat, near the drawbridge. And now the boy shifted the light to the bottom of the moat, and we could see the missing Mary Mae Milgrim.

She was lying at the bottom of the moat. And I knew by the way her neck was twisted that Mary Mae Milgrim was dead.

══════════ *FOUR* ══════════

LIEUTENANT REMINGTON, FROM Beverly Hills Headquarters, brought Sergeant Gnup with him and another detective I didn't know, plus three uniformed men. Lieutenant Remington was home-grown and Mary Mae Milgrim was still a big name to him.

Nobody was permitted to leave. The courtyard lights were turned on and all the guests were assembled in the ballroom. Lieutenant Remington stayed outside with Aunt Sheila and the Japanese boy; they had found the body.

In the ballroom, Homer fumed and fretted. "What's the matter with that lieutenant?" he asked me. "He doesn't suspect Sheila, does he?"

"He suspects everybody who is here, if it was murder," I said. "It hasn't been established as murder yet. She could easily have gone outside for some air and fallen into the moat. The cause of death hasn't been determined."

"Well," he said, "if it turns out to be murder, I want you to work on it, Brock."

I stared at him.

"I'll pay for it," he said. "If it's murder, I want the killer caught."

"Homer," I asked patiently, "why—?"

"I always enjoyed her," he said. "She gave me many happy hours." He seemed embarrassed. "Damn it, it's the *least* I can do." He put a hand on my arm. "Just don't tell your aunt who's paying you. She's sure as hell getting stingy with *my* money."

Then my old semi-friend, Sergeant Gnup, was bustling over in his officious and official way.

"You," he greeted me. "Now, what in hell are *you* doing here?"

"He is my guest," Homer said firmly. "And who are you?"

I introduced them. I told Sergeant Gnup, "Mr. Gallup is the host. He bought this house from Miss Milgrim and tonight's party was planned as a housewarming. Mr. Gallup is married to my aunt."

"Well, well," Gnup said. "Cozy, huh?"

"Translate that into English," I said.

He looked doubtfully at Homer and belligerently at me. "The word I get so far is that Mrs. Gallup went out to look for Miss Milgrim with blood in her eye."

Homer glared at him; I kept my face bland. Neither of us said anything.

"So what was the fight about?" Gnup asked.

I said calmly, "Sergeant, when my aunt found Miss Milgrim, she was accompanied by a servant. I imagine you have questioned him?"

"I haven't. He's out there with the Lieutenant. You telling me my business, Callahan?"

"Someone should," I said quietly. "If you have questions, ask them. If you have accusations, save them until we're booked."

His face reddened and his soft, flattened nose twitched pugnaciously. "I've told you before, Irish. Watch your lip."

Next to me, Homer was rigid as stone. "Sergeant," he said ominously, "you're in my home. I will stand for no insolence. Keep your voice down and your tongue civil or *leave!*"

Gnup stared at him.

"I know you're a police officer," Homer told him, "but I'm a citizen and you're on my property. Now, we're all going to co-operate—*but we will not be intimidated.*"

That Homer. . . . My kind of bastard.

Gnup took a deep breath of air. Gnup looked at two hundred-and-twenty-pound me, two-hundred-and-fifteen-pound Homer and at some unoccupied air between us.

Finally he said, "Why was Mrs. Gallup looking for Miss Milgrim?"

"To tell her off," Homer said honestly. "My wife thought Miss Milgrim had cheated her on this house. However, that wasn't possible. I was informed by the broker I could make a smaller offer than I did. I didn't want to haggle with Miss Milgrim."

"And why not?"

"I happen to be one of her fans."

I asked, "Has the cause of death been determined? You're making this sound like a murder investigation, Sergeant."

"That's the way it's going to sound until we find out it isn't," Gnup said. "I'm talking to Mr. Gallup, Callahan. Stay out of this." He turned back to Homer. "Who was the broker?"

"His name is Darrow, Wallace Darrow," Homer said. "He's here tonight."

Gnup frowned. "The broker is here? Friend of yours, is he?"

"Not exactly. I don't know many people in town, so my wife invited him."

"*You* didn't?"

Homer shook his head. "She told me she was going to and I approved. After all, he found me this wonderful house."

"You think you got a good buy then?"

Homer smiled. "Look around you, at this magnificent room. The whole joint for a hundred and forty thousand, man. I stole it."

Gnup said stubbornly, "At eighty-five thousand it would have been a better bargain, wouldn't it?"

"Possibly," Homer admitted. "But I'm not a business-man, Sergeant. I made a few dollars in oil, but business shenanigans bore me."

Gnup took another breath. "Mr. Gallup, to *most people*, fifty-five thousand dollars is a lot of money. A hell of a lot of money. And they would resent being overcharged that much."

Homer nodded. "I'm sure you're right, Sergeant. But I don't happen to be *most people*. I happen to be a big shot from Gila Creek." He winked at me. "And that ain't easy, coming from Gila Creek."

Gnup's soft nose twitched again and his voice was quiet. "Perhaps your wife didn't take quite as tolerant a view about being overcharged fifty-five thousand dollars?"

"She sure as hell didn't," Homer admitted innocently. "But she knows I love Mary Mae and she sure as hell wouldn't harm her."

Gnup stared. "You were in love with Miss Milgrim?"

Homer returned the stare. "Hell, yes! Weren't you? Wasn't *everybody?*"

Gnup shook his head and stared sullenly between us. He said to me, "You found a soul mate, didn't you? Stay here, both of you; I'll be back." He went over toward where another detective was talking with Joyce Thorne.

"Cantankerous fellow, isn't he?" Homer said.

I nodded, watching Joyce Thorne.

Homer asked quietly, "She couldn't have been murdered, could she? What *reason* could anyone have?"

"Money, for one," I said. "Mary Mae was a lot richer than she liked to admit, Homer."

"And was the heir here? Or the heirs? Who gets it?"

"I have no idea. I was just giving you one reason for murder. There are a lot of others. But we don't know that it was murder yet, do we?"

Homer looked bleakly out at his guests. "No, but I've got a bad feeling it was. Mary Mae—" He sighed. "What kind of animal would kill Mary Mae?"

Outside, there was a peal of thunder. We get rain out here in the spring, but rarely thunder. A murmur moved through the nervous crowd in the ballroom. A siren wailed and Lieutenant Remington came into the room from the archway that led to the entry hall. The Japanese servant was with him.

"Where the hell's Sheila?" Homer asked. "Do you think they took her down to the station?"

"No," I answered. "Easy now, Homer." I went over to intercept the Lieutenant.

He grimaced impatiently as I approached. "Keep out of my hair, Callahan. I've already had enough trouble with your aunt."

"All I want to know is where she is, Lieutenant."

"She's on her way to Headquarters, that's where she is. She's even more insolent than you are." He brushed past me.

Homer had followed me over, and he had heard the conversation. He tried to grab Remington's arm but Remington brushed past him too. He said to me, "Get an attorney. I'm going down there. I'll meet you down there."

"I doubt if the police will let you leave, Homer," I warned him. "Let me ask the Lieutenant about it."

"Call an attorney," he said. "Don't worry about me."

I went to look for a phone to call Tommy Self.

In Lieutenant Remington's office, Tommy conversed quietly with Homer, out of my audio range. Though he had gone to Stanford with me, and quarterbacked our team,

Tommy had gone to Harvard after that and become a little pretentious.

He hadn't wanted to come down until I told him Homer was my aunt's latest husband. Tommy knew that Aunt Sheila never settled for the middle class.

And now he was giving Homer all the well-bred attention Harvard lawyers reserve for wealthy Texans. Lieutenant Remington and Sergeant Gnup were questioning a few of the selected guests in another room.

Somewhere, I sensed, they had uncovered a potentially revealing line of investigation. It was possible that they knew most of the old local residents rather intimately, particularly the cinema crowd, and were familiar with most of the feuds and alliances.

The door opened and Lieutenant Remington came in with the Japanese servant.

Tommy stood up and Remington said, "Mrs. Gallup claims you are also here to represent Mr. Yoshida. Is that true?"

Homer said, "Of course it's true. Do you think my wife's a liar?"

Remington looked coolly at Homer. "I was addressing Mr. Self, sir."

"And talking about *my* wife," Homer reminded him. "Mr. Self will represent Mr. Yoshida."

Lieutenant Remington gave Homer a long, hard look and then went over to sit behind his desk. Yoshida came over to sit next to me on the leather couch.

"Callahan's my name," I told him. "Brock Callahan."

"I know," he said softly. "I've seen you many times, the greatest guard who ever played football. My name is Raymond Yoshida."

We shook hands and I looked up to meet Lieutenant Remington's stare.

"Soliciting?" he asked me. "Business slow?"

"I never solicit, Lieutenant," I said with dignity.

He made some comment I couldn't hear. Anger stirred in me, but my mouth remained shut.

Homer, my good friend, said, "Mr. Callahan doesn't need to solicit. He's working for me on this case."

Remington's eyebrows lifted. He smiled disdainfully.

I continued to keep my mouth shut, but the smile had got to Homer. He said acidly, "With what I've seen tonight, it's plain to me an *efficient* investigator is needed."

Tommy murmured something to Homer and Remington looked rigidly at both of them. Silence. Next to me, Raymond Yoshida stirred uncomfortably. I yawned.

It was one of those high-tension silences that sometimes precede vocal thunder. And then an interruption broke the moment's tension. Aunt Sheila came through the doorway talking a mile a minute, Gnup trailing her.

She glared at Remington and he said curtly, "Please be seated, Mrs. Gallup."

Aunt Sheila came over to crowd in next to me. Sergeant Gnup looked around and saw no empty seats. He stood against the wall next to Remington's chair.

I asked politely, "Has the cause of death been determined, Lieutenant?"

He nodded. "Would you like to guess at what it was?"

I shook my head.

"Try," he said.

"Well, by the way her neck was twisted, a fall might have done it."

He shook his head but didn't enlighten me.

Aunt Sheila said, "She was poisoned. With coniine. What's coniine, Brock?"

An alkaloid, I thought, *contained in Conium maculatum. And the common name for Conium maculatum is poison hemlock*. I thought back a few days to my fan behind the counter who had taken my order. As a gag, I had ordered hemlock. I shivered.

Remington said, "What are you thinking about, Callahan? You look nervous. What's on your mind, Callahan? Quick!"

I ignored him. I said to Aunt Sheila, "Coniine is a poison soluble in alcohol." Then I looked at Remington. "I was thinking of hemlock, Lieutenant. I was thinking of Socrates."

His face stiffened.

I said soothingly, "For some reason, we've all got off to a bad start. If you don't feel, Lieutenant, that my services would be of any help to the Department, I won't accept Mr. Gallup as a client in this case."

Homer started to object, but Tommy Self quickly put a hand on his arm. Remington looked at Gnup.

Gnup said, "Callahan and I aren't exactly buddies, but we have no reason to distrust him, Lieutenant."

Remington leaned back in his chair and took a deep breath. After a thoughtful moment, he said, "It has been a bad start." He looked levelly at Aunt Sheila. "Triggered by considerable citizen arrogance."

Aunt Sheila said nothing. Her face showed nothing.

Tommy said, "I'm sure Mrs. Gallup was horribly shocked by what she discovered. It was bound to react unfavorably on her—disposition."

"And she hasn't got the best disposition in the world to begin with," I added.

Gnup laughed. Remington almost smiled.

The door opened again and a uniformed man said, "A Miss Bonnet wants to know if she may come in, Lieutenant. She's a friend of Mrs. Gallup."

"It's my girl," I said. "I'll go out with her and wait in the hall. Okay?"

Remington nodded. Almost thankfully, I thought. Gnup came over to take the seat I was vacating. There seemed to be less tension in the room when I left.

In the hall, Jan said, "What's going on in there? What kind of a ridiculous police department is this?"

"Simmer down," I said. "Aunt Sheila, as usual, was talking when she should have been listening. I'd have run her in myself."

"I'll bet you would. And you'd have let me sit out here the rest of the night, I suppose, if I hadn't made a fuss?"

"There was no reason for you to come," I said. "Let's go out and get some air."

"It's raining," she said. "What's going on in there?"

"A conference. It's going to be all right. Now, damn it, calm down! It's none of your business."

She stared at me. "Well—! Since when are you such a great defender of the police?"

"Always," I informed her. "They take too much and get paid too little for it. They don't always like me, but I've always had a great respect for conscientious police officers."

The door had opened while I was talking, and Sergeant Gnup came through to hear the last part of my speech. "Glad to hear it," he said dryly. "Could I have a word or two in private?"

Jan sniffed and went down to the other end of the hall. Gnup said quietly, "Remington is glad to have you on it; don't worry about that. He's just had a bad evening is all. Look, check out this Joyce Thorne woman tomorrow, huh? Tonight, we've had it. We're going to stay here and consolidate what we have, and we'll brief you in the morning on that. Got me?"

"Got you, Sergeant," I said. "I suppose my aunt will be released?"

He nodded. ''The Lieutenant was miffed and lost his head for a second there. She's—not easy to get along with, your aunt.''

I agreed she wasn't and promised to see him in the morning. I went down to where Jan was waiting.

''Aunt Sheila will be released soon,'' I told her. ''I suppose the party is over?''

''Definitely. Do we have to wait for them?''

''Don't you want to?''

''I suppose it would be rude, but I want to be alone, with you.''

Mercurial Jan . . . . I wondered if I had read her right. I asked shakily. ''Alone? Where?''

''My place,'' she said. ''Alone with you, at my place.''

I took her hand and we went out into the soft rain.

FIVE

THE RAIN KEPT coming down. Next to me, on her big bed, Jan dozed restlessly. It had been a strange encounter, passive, suppliant at first. And then murmurings and trembling and clutching co-operation and a choked cry at culmination. With a few tears.

The beat of the rain grew heavier and the gurgle from the eave troughs louder. Jan stirred and asked dreamily, "Can't you sleep?"

"No."

"What are you thinking about?"

"About you and me. About Mary Mae Milgrim and my Aunt Sheila."

"What were you thinking about us?"

"About what a dead end we're in. We'll never be married, not to each other."

"I don't want to think about it, not tonight."

"Okay." I turned over and stretched.

Oblivion had almost drowned me when she asked, "What do you mean—dead end?"

"You know what I mean. You won't marry a poor man and I won't run my profession like a rich man. We're dead-ended; we're hanging onto a hopeless hope."

She sighed and stretched. "Tomorrow," she said. "We'll talk about it tomorrow."

There weren't enough tomorrows. There were too many yesterdays and not enough tomorrows. But who could convince Jan of that? She made a living off the glamour trade; reality lived off her street.

The rain was a downpour now, and again there was that rare sound of thunder. Jan stirred, murmuring in her sleep.

Down, down, down came the rain, finally bringing oblivion to me.

In the morning, the *Times* gave the Mary Mae Milgrim death complete coverage. There was a full page of pictures, mostly stills in roles that had brought her fame.

Some pictures must have been shot at the party after I had left. John Davenport and Enrico Rivali were shown at one of the bars and there was a shot of Scooter Calvin with Joyce Thorne. Raymond Yoshida was identified as a servant of Mary Mae's; I had assumed he had been hired only for the party. He was a gardener.

There were a number of quotes from the ancient stars who had attended the party, a last pathetic effort to get some ink in a world that had forgotten them. All of them had identified themselves as "Mary Mae's best friend."

No one had identified himself as an enemy, but it seemed plain there must have been at least one. How many of them, however, would know how to acquire a lethal does of coniine? Someone with a chemist friend?

"It's shocking, isn't it?" Jan asked. "All her friends looked so—so resigned, defeated. And yet one of them must have retained enough animosity to kill."

"Nobody," I said, "has mentioned the possibility of suicide."

"Suicide—?" Jan stared in wonder. "What made you think of that?"

"Nothing, really. Except that everyone else seems to have completely overlooked it. And I would guess eighty

per cent of all premeditated poisoning deaths are self-in-
flicted."

"If you know that, the police must know it. They don't
tell everything they know to the newspapers, do they?"

"Not in Beverly Hills. But still, those police reporters
should have thought of it. I suppose the magic of Mary Mae
Milgrim is still powerful down on First Street. It isn't the
first name they've covered for."

Jan sipped her coffee and turned to the society pages. All
the crimes bored her except the crime of bad taste. Perhaps
I misjudged her; perhaps it was fright more than boredom
that kept her out of the other pages. Unless I was involved
in a case, I rarely looked at anything but the sports pages.

Lieutenant Remington was quoted as stating a potentially
revealing line of inquiry had been opened and his hopes for
success were optimistic. He hadn't seemed optimistic to me
when I had left him last night. This was possibly only a
quote for the taxpayers.

I finished my coffee and kissed my girl and went down
to see Sergeant Gnup.

He was in a room next to Lieutenant Remington's office,
talking with some reporters for the afternoon Los Angeles
papers and one reporter from the *Beverly Hills Bugle*.

I took one look at all of them and closed the door quietly
again. I went down the hall to Lieutenant Remington's office.

He looked up from his desk and frowned. "Sergeant
Gnup busy?"

"With the vultures of the press," I agreed. "I dropped
in to learn what this 'potentially revealing line of inquiry'
is that you were quoted about in this morning's *Times*."

He sighed. "Sit down. I'll be with you in a minute."

I sat patiently and humbly in the chair on the other side
of his desk and watched him sign some papers and read a

few reports. He was probably hamming it up a little in order to establish my lowly place in *his* scheme of things.

When he had milked the scene dry, he looked up thoughtfully and said, "Our revealing line of inquiry would be Joyce Thorne. Unfortunately, this Department hasn't the men or the time to completely investigate her background and—and alliances without outside help."

"And that's where Callahan comes in?"

He nodded and fiddled with a ball-point pen on his desk.

"An interesting assignment," I said. "Are you embarrassed, Lieutenant Remington?"

His face showed his annoyance. "Embarrassed? Why should I be?"

"I don't know. You seemed embarrassed. What is so special about Joyce Thorne?"

"We have private information. It is not for publication yet. The information we have will have to be made public at the proper time by Miss Milgrim's attorneys."

I stared at him. "Are you telling me that Miss Thorne is one of Miss Milgrim's heirs?"

"The *only* heir," Remington said. "And the estate is—impressive.

I shook my head. "Well, I'll be dammed!"

"Miss Thorne has not been informed as yet," Remington went on. "We hope to withhold the information as long as we can. And I'm thinking that you're the wrong man to investigate *her*."

"Because of her body or the boodle, Lieutenant?"

He didn't answer.

"I'm not a lecher," I said. "I'm not Joe Puma. I'm a square, Lieutenant, poor and honest. Occasionally, I am a victim of my strong romantic compulsions, but I have never accepted a dishonest dollar."

He leaned back in his chair and stared at the top of his desk.

"If you really didn't trust me," I pointed out, "you wouldn't have told me the secret that only you and her attorneys know right now. Something else must be eating you, Lieutenant."

His eyes came up to meet mine. "Yes. You'll be working for Homer Gallup. Does that mean you'll also be protecting him?"

"From what? How could Mr. Gallup be involved? He bought that house at Miss Milgrim's asking price only because of sentiment, because he wouldn't think of haggling with his idol."

"Is that so? He was very sure, however, to get all mineral rights in the property, wasn't he? Are you trying to tell me an oil man doesn't know that geologists considered that area very promising?"

I said nothing. This was all news to me.

"Do you think he really wanted that place as a *home?*" Remington asked quietly. "The people in that area have kept the oil men out of there for years. Because *they* think of it as a place for a *home*. Do you think that was Gallup's only concern?"

"Yes," I said honestly. "As a matter of fact, a friend of mine is already preparing to completely redecorate the place."

"Miss Bonnet?"

I nodded.

He chewed his lower lip.

I said, "Even if he had planned to drill there, what possible reason could he have for killing Miss Milgrim? The property was in escrow, soon to be delivered to Mr. Gallup."

"With one reservation," Remington said. "So long as she was alive, Miss Milgrim was to retain free occupancy of that gardener's cottage on the place. And so long as she retained occupancy, *there was to be no oil well drilling.*"

Again, I said nothing. Again, he had pulled me out of the dark into the frightening light.

My mind went back to Cini's, when Jan had called Darrow.

"No," I said. "Lieutenant, it was only a coincidence that Homer Gallup happened to be shown Mary Mae Milgrim's house. He was shown a number of others, first, but they were too modern for him."

"Is that so? I happen to know that he admired that house long before Wallace Darrow ever showed it to him."

This was turning into the day of revelation. I was speechless for the third time.

"You really are an innocent," Remington said scornfully. "How in hell do you think a man gets to be a millionaire? By being jovial, by throwing parties and picking up tabs and slapping his friends on the back? Do you think that outsized Rotarian image he's built in your mind is *real?*"

I gulped, and remained silent.

Remington shook his head wonderingly. "And Sergeant Gnup thinks you're a cynical man."

"I'm not. But I think you're way off base on Homer Gallup. Who told you he'd seen that house before?"

"Darrow. He said that he and Homer were alone for a few minutes when they were going through those other houses, and Homer asked him if it was true the Milgrim house was for sale. Darrow said it was and Homer told him not to tell your aunt it was his idea, but to show them that house. Then Darrow passed the buck to Miss Bonnet, he claims, and *she* suggested looking at the Milgrim place."

Jan, my Jan. . . .She hadn't said a word to me about this. . . .

"Well—?" Remington asked.

I shrugged.

"What are you thinking?"

I sighed. "I'm thinking nothing is *ever* the way it seems, is it?"

He didn't answer. He turned silent again and stared at the top of his desk.

"And now," I guessed, "you don't trust me, either."

He gave it some thought and finally made a decision. He looked up and faced me as squarely as a con man. "I trust you, Brock. You keep us informed, every day."

They needed me. They hated to admit it, but they needed me. I rose and said with simple dignity, "Every day. We'll lick this thing, Lieutenant." I gave it the proper pause and added, "Together."

I thought he winced, but I pretended not to notice. I bowed gracefully and left him with his thoughts.

The logical place to head for was the gardener's cottage still occupied by Joyce Thorne. But I had another mission first. I headed for a place nearby, the working base of my semi-true love.

The door was wormwood and the uncapitalized black script on the shining show window read *jan bonnet—interiors*.

She was in the rear of the shop, showing some damask fabric to a bulky dowager, when I entered. She nodded to me and continued to give her attention to her client (customer).

I sat on a fragile gilt chair and pretended to be absorbed in a trade magazine.

The dowager left eventually, promising to return after she had talked with her husband. Jan came back from the doorway to stand in front of me.

I looked up from the magazine and said, "My own true love."

She took a breath. "You've talked with Wallace Darrow, I'd guess."

I shook my head. "But I have his story. You and he conned my poor Aunt Sheila, didn't you?"

She closed her eyes wearily. She opened them and said, "Brock, Homer wanted that house so badly he could taste it. What could I do? He has a right to his own impossible taste, hasn't he? What was I supposed to do?"

"The least you could have done was confide in me," I answered. "Why didn't you?"

"And have you go blabbing it all to your Aunt Sheila? What would she think of me?"

"She'd have thought a little more of you than she's going to, finding it out this late."

Jan stared. "You mean you're going to tell her—*now?*"

"I'm sure the police are. Because, you see, the police don't believe Homer wanted that house to live in. They think he wanted it for the possible oil under it." I told her what Remington had told me.

When I had finished, she said, "That's ridiculous! That's absurd! How could they think such horrible thoughts about such a *nice* man?"

"Maybe he's not a *nice* man," I said. "Maybe he's only a *rich* man. In your lexicon, the words might be synonymous, but the police don't take quite the same innocent view of it."

Her soft brown eyes flared. "Watch it—! Watch your nasty damned tongue, Brock Callahan."

I stood up. "Don't take out your sense of guilt on me. I think what you did was inexcusable."

Silence, while her eyes grew harder and harder. Then she said, "Get out. Get out right now. And don't come back!"

"I'll wait for your call," I told her. "And when the time comes, I'll probably accept your apology."

"Go—!" she shrieked, and I went.

The rain had washed the streets and dispelled the inversion

that gives us our smog. I turned the flivver toward Sunset Boulevard and the temporary domicile of Joyce Thorne.

She was home this clear morning. There were no traces of grief on her face, though her manner was sober, her voice soft and her dress black. The black dress and the jet hair accentuated the warm ivory of her complexion. She was no sun worshiper, this one; she was all woman.

The living room was raftered and the longest wall afforded a vast view of Beverly Hills.

"These servants lived well," I commented.

She smiled distantly and indicated a chintzy upholstered chair.

I sat down and looked out at the view. Without turning my head, I said, "Have the police been a nuisance?"

"Nuisance?" Pause. "I wouldn't say they were exactly that. They questioned me—rather stubbornly, I thought, and went over the same ground again and again. But I suppose that's all part of their jobs."

"When is the funeral?" I asked.

"There will be no public service," Miss Thorne said quietly. "Her attorneys have already told me she wished to be cremated."

I turned to look at her. "You've been in touch with them?"

Her deep blue eyes met mine candidly. "Yes. Why are you surprised?"

"I'm not. Did I look surprised?"

"You looked more than that. You looked—startled." She sat on an upholstered love seat nearby and faced me. "Mr. Callahan, why are you here? Certainly not to learn when the funeral is to be, or how much trouble the police have given me. Are you working on this case?"

I nodded. "In co-operation with the Beverly Hills Police Department."

"But *for* your Aunt? To protect her, is that right?"

I shook my head emphatically. "Why should my aunt need protection?"

"Isn't she the logical suspect? Who else is there?" Her voice was less soft.

"According to—one of my informants, there was a whole room full of Miss Milgrim's enemies at the party."

"That's—absurd!" Color came to the flawless cheeks. "Who would say a horrible thing like that?"

"Someone in a position to know. Miss Thorne, there aren't any favorite suspects at the moment. As the people are questioned, and start to tell lies, a pattern will eventually emerge. Until that time, everyone at the party and a number of people who weren't officially there will *all* be suspects."

"Lies—?" she asked. "What kind of lies?"

"All the kinds. Some by the innocent and some by the involved. People lie for a variety of reasons and the reasons have to be sorted and the lies fitted into the puzzle. It's a complicated business, but the police understand it very well."

A long, long silence. And then she asked, "How could I be a suspect? I loved Miss Milgrim. What reason could I have for harming Miss Milgrim?"

I shrugged. "If she left any estate worth mentioning, you could be one of the heirs. Did she have any relatives?"

"Only a brother she hasn't seen for twenty years. He lives in Florida."

"He was notified, of course?"

She nodded. "He—didn't approve of Miss Milgrim. I imagine she left her money to charity."

"Was she well-to-do?"

"She was rich." Her voice was a whisper. "She was very careful with her money. And she made it in the days before income taxes were high. It must be an enormous estate."

I asked casually, "How did you happen to go to work for her?"

She expelled her breath. "My parents knew her. She was a very good friend of my mother's. I had some—theatrical ambitions and Miss Milgrim suggested I come to work as her secretary and companion and in that way meet some people who might do me some good theatrically."

"I see. Are your parents local people?"

She nodded, looking out at the hills. "They live in Santa Monica."

"You'll be going back to them now, will you?"

There was a trace of belligerence in her face. "No. Mr. Gallup told me I could stay here as long as I wanted to. I like it here."

"Rent free?" I asked.

She stared at me angrily and said nothing.

I, too, said nothing. But thought, *Wait until my Aunt Sheila hears about this.* There would be fireworks. Poor Homer. . . .

Joyce Thorne's deadly level voice broke through my reverie. "I think I've answered enough questions for today. I—don't like to be rude, but I have things to do."

She didn't go to the door with me. Twice in an hour I had been sent away by women, first Jan and now Miss Thorne. I went out into the clear day feeling rejected.

From a shrub he was pruning near the doorway, Raymond Yoshida looked up, saw me, and came over. "Could I speak with you alone?" he asked me.

"Of course. Here?"

He shook his head. "I have a room over the garage. Mr. Gallup wants me to stay on."

"Lead the way," I said.

SIX

WHAT HE HAD called a room was in reality an apartment and a hell of a lot bigger and nicer than my Westwood rattrap. It, like the servants' cottage, had a story-and-a-half raftered living room with a view of the city through a bank of windows on the longest wall.

"You live well," I said.

"I'm a first-class gardener," he told me, "and can double as a waiter. I should live well."

I didn't live this well. Was I a second-class investigator? I asked him, "What did you want to tell me?"

"About Enrico Rivali. About a conversation I overheard between him and Miss Milgrim."

"I'm all ears, Raymond."

"It was about three weeks ago," Yoshida went on. "They were standing next to the fountain there, and I was mulching some flower beds on the other side of those junipers. They were—really hollering at each other. And then Rivali said, 'You'd be nothing without me. Nothing! So, remember I made you and I can destroy you.' And Miss Milgrim told him to go to hell."

"And that's all?"

"Not quite. Rivali said something else, something I didn't hear, and Miss Milgrim said, 'Nobody would believe you, anyway. And I'd sue you, and what could you prove?' And then they talked quieter for a while and then he left.''

"Has Rivali been a frequent visitor here?"

"Every day since I've been here," Yoshida told me, "and I've been here three years. I guess it's been going on forever."

"How does Rivali live? Has he an income?"

Yoshida shrugged. "I don't know for sure, but a wild guess would be that Miss Milgrim was his income. I couldn't prove that. Maybe I only say it because I don't like him."

There was a silence, and then I asked him, "How old are you?"

"Twenty-seven. Why?"

"You look younger. I thought you were just a kid."

He smiled. "Thank you. You look younger too. You look young enough to still be with the Rams."

I thanked him for the compliment and for the information and went back to my car. From the side yard of the cottage, Joyce Thorne watched me over the top of a magazine she pretended to be reading. She had sent me away because she had things to do, urgent things like reading a magazine.

Behind me, the battlements and turrets of the Gallup castle were bathed in the clear noon sun. I drove out, over the drawbridge, and headed for the drugstore near my office.

From behind the lunch counter, my fan looked at me compassionately. "Bad morning?"

"Unproductive. Was I scowling?"

"You were looking beat. We've got some first-class clam chowder. Not canned, either. We got a new cook."

"I'll try it," I said.

He smiled and winked and went to get my order. My one stable friend, always loyal, always cordial. . . . We had established an almost perfect empathy and I still didn't know his name.

Next to me, a dowager spooned greedily into a banana split and read sadly about Mary Mae Milgrim. Her eyes were wet and there was some chocolate syrup on her chin.

There would be tears for Mary Mae but probably not many from those close to her. And what would the mourners mourn, the death of Mary Mae or their own youth?

A big man took the stool next to mine, a big man named Homer Gallup. He said, "I saw your car in the parking lot but you weren't in the office, so I came here. Is the food any good?"

"For the price, it's all right. You look depressed, Homer."

"I've been thinking about Miss Milgrim," he said. "It really didn't hit home last night; I had too much booze in me. But it's been a bad morning."

I said nothing. The police suspicion of him was something I was not ethically free to voice, even if he was my newest uncle.

He said it for me. "I've been with Lieutenant Remington for over an hour. You know, I think that bastard is suspicious of *me?* He was even talking about oil, as though I hadn't bought that place for a home."

"Oil?" I asked, in bewildered pseudo-innocence.

"Oil," he repeated wearily. "Ye gods, I've got half my wells out of production now to keep down my income. What in hell would I do with more oil?"

I chuckled.

"What's funny?" he asked irritatedly.

"A man with too much money," I explained. "No man can have too much money, can he?"

"Not while those socialists are running the country, no. They'll see to that."

My fan brought my clam chowder and Homer ordered a bowl of it. And asked me, "Why didn't he bring me a cup of coffee? In Texas, they bring you a cup of coffee and *then* take your order."

"A lot of people in Beverly Hills drink tea," I explained. "It's a strange town."

"Don't I know it?" he said. "I've had reason to look up a couple credit ratings." He sighed. "But your Aunt Sheila would never settle for Texas, would she?"

I shrugged. "Maybe, if you bought a place close enough to Neiman-Marcus—"

He laughed. He put a hand on my shoulder. "Damn it, I'm glad I found you. Brock, you're my all-time favorite nephew, I don't mind telling you."

And then my fan, who has big ears, set a cup of coffee in front of Homer and said, "I waited for a fresh pot, sir."

Homer smiled and sighed. "This day is getting better every minute. You play golf, Brock?"

"Not today," I said. "Not until we find out who killed Miss Milgrim, Homer."

He nodded and sipped his coffee. He asked quietly, "Any progress?"

"Very little," I said. Though he was my client, I didn't think I was free to tell him about Joyce Thorne, heiress. I asked, "Is it true you're letting Miss Thorne stay there indefinitely?"

He nodded.

"Rent free?"

He nodded again and stared at me. "Why not? Do I need the rent?"

"No. But in the interests of domestic peace, don't you think it would be wise to tell Aunt Sheila that Miss Thorne is paying rent?"

"I've already lied to Sheila about that," he admitted.

His chowder came and he began to eat.

I said, "Raymond Yoshida told me he's staying on too."

"That's right. Your aunt's idea. She thinks he's a first-class gardener." He looked at me. "You been over to the house this morning?"

"To talk with Yoshida. He told me—this Rivali was threatening Miss Milgrim. Do you remember Rivali from the party, Enrico Rivali?"

"Hell, yes. He bent my ear for almost an hour, trying to get me to finance a picture for Mary Mae. Somehow, I don't like him. He looks—sly."

"Yoshida doesn't like him either. Did Rivali give you a card or anything? Do you know where he lives?"

Homer reached into a jacket pocket and took out a small notebook. He leafed through it until he found what he wanted, tore out the page and handed it to me.

Under Rivali's name was an address and phone number. The address was in Brentwood.

Homer said, "You check him out good, Brock. He's a sharp one; he's got all the makings of a con man." Homer glowered. "Threatening Miss Milgrim, was he? Hmmmmph!"

"Homer," I said gently, "Miss Milgrim might not have been quite the sweet and gullible dove she portrayed in her pictures. It's possible the money you're spending to find her murderer will only degrade the picture of her you have in your mind."

"You find him," he said brusquely.

"I mean to try. Also, there is still a possibility she committed suicide. I'm going to check with her doctor and find out about her health."

He nodded. He called my fan over and ordered another bowl of clam chowder. He wiped his mouth and said, "Maybe she wasn't any angel but she was a damned fine actress and I don't think the cops in this town could find a load of manure in a phone booth."

I didn't argue with him any further. What was a lousy hundred dollars a day to him?

After he'd left, I phoned Lieutenant Remington and asked if Miss Milgrim's doctor had been questioned regarding her health.

"Because of the suicide angle? Hell, yes. And I'd say there wasn't one chance in a million that it was suicide. What have you been doing this morning?"

"I talked with Miss Thorne and that gardener, Yoshida. Now, I'm on my way to talk with Enrico Rivali."

"Learn anything?"

"Nothing startling. I had lunch with my client. Is he still on your list?"

"Right. As a matter of fact, everyone who was at the party is still on *my* list. Even you. Carry on." He hung up.

That last crack had been pointless and arrogant. I went out, nettled, and climbed into the flivver.

Brentwood is considered one of the better districts in the Los Angeles area, but it has its seamier side, near the Veterans' Administration grounds. On the borderline between this near-slum and the finer homes was the address of Enrico Rivali.

It was a small, thick-walled Spanish place with a heavy tile roof. The front yard was all succulents and gravel, and untrimmed growth of cacti, jade plant and flowering ice plant. Bougainvillaea shrouded the narrow, one-car garage and hung over the open doorway. There was an ancient Packard in the garage.

The sound of the door chimes reverberated through the small house and then the darkly stained door opened and I was looking at the sallow, unfriendly face of Enrico Rivali.

"You—" he said. "What the hell do you want?"

"A few words of private conversation. I'm working with the Beverly Hills Police Department on the death of Miss Milgrim."

"This isn't Beverly Hills," he said. "This is Los Angeles." He started to close the door.

"One second," I said sharply.

He paused, the door half-closed.

"A little co-operation isn't going to hurt you," I said mildly. "I have friends in the Los Angeles Department too, but I didn't think it would be necessary to bring them. Also, I am licensed by the state and my activities are not confined to Beverly Hills."

"Last time we talked, you threatened me," he said gratingly.

I shook my head. "Not quite. I asked you to lay off my uncle."

He frowned. "Uncle? I thought you called him a friend?"

"He's both," I explained. "He's married to my aunt." I paused. "My only aunt."

Another moment of hesitation while his cunning mind digested that. Then he held the door wider and said grudgingly, "Okay. Come on in."

I came into a small entry hall and from there into the living room. The windows were narrow, with deep sills, and the furniture looked like castoffs from the Milgrim mansion. I sat on a dark velour davenport while he sat on an upholstered, wrought-iron bench near the tiny fireplace.

He didn't look at me. "Miss Thorne is still staying out there, I heard.'

"That's right. My uncle is a generous man. Mr. Rivali, if Miss Milgrim had any really malignant enemies, you'd know them, I'm sure."

"I'm sure I would too. But I don't happen to be a gossip."

I said evenly, "I'm not asking for gossip. I'm asking for what might be leads in a murder case. I happen to know that you threatened Miss Milgrim and I should think you'd be anxious to relieve any suspicion of yourself."

His narrow face stiffened.

"In the event," I went on blithely, "that you are innocent of any involvement."

"The police," he said, "have already questioned me." He stood up. "You'd better go."

"Not yet," I told him. "I'm a *private* operative, Mr. Rivali, and interested only in the information that might lead me to a killer. You can be perfectly frank with me. Discretion is part of what I sell."

"Get out!" he said, and his voice was harsh.

I shook my head.

There was the sound of a footstep to my right and I glanced that way. A big, ugly man stood in the archway to the entry hall, a man with a cauliflower ear and dimly familiar face.

"Trouble, Ricky?" the big man asked quietly.

I remembered him then, a former local wrestler who had played bit parts as a heavy in a host of B pictures.

Enrico (Ricky) Rivali said, "No trouble, George. Mr. Callahan is leaving."

George Parkas, that was the man's name. I smiled at him and looked back at Rivali. "I'm not leaving. You're being stupid about this."

"You are leaving," George Parkas said from the doorway.

"Go away," I told him. "You're big but you're old and you were never much. Go away before you are forced to make an ass of yourself."

Enrico was smiling now. "George isn't old. George is only fifty. And strong as an ox."

"Send him away," I said, and my hands trembled. "I have an adolescent reaction to physical threat and I don't want to humiliate an old man. Send him away, Rivali."

George muttered something and took a step into the room, his arms in the bowed, hanging position of the advancing wrestler.

I didn't get up. I stared between him and Rivali and back and said, "Don't start anything. You're not that far into the clear, Rivali. Co-operation is still your safest course.''

They smiled at each other and I knew why Rivali had never married. And the conversational persiflage about girls at the party had been fraudulent. These two had found each other.

"I'll open the door," Rivali said to George, "and you can throw him out from this end of the hall. Do you think he'll bounce?"

George smiled in his nitwitted way and came slowly over to where I was still seated. He stood in front of me, leaning forward.

"I'll get the door," Rivali said, and started to leave the room as George leaned forward and reached for me.

My stout right leg came up, and I braced my back into the davenport as I let George have it. Not where it hurts the most; I had no intention of doing him permanent damage. My foot found purchase higher, flat against his ribbed belly.

His long arms had almost reached my neck when I straightened my knee and put him into orbit. He went backward with the speed of light and crashed into the wrought-iron bench next to the fireplace; and then his head went into the imitation marble of the mantel with a ''*thunk*''that made the windows rattle.

He was unconscious before he reached the floor.

And Rivali came at me like a cat, shrieking and spitting, his fingernails clawing toward my face.

I knocked him halfway across the room with the back of my hand and stood up to meet his next charge.

There was none. He was bending over George, sobbing and solicitous, when I went out.

ഐഐഐഐഐ SEVEN ഐഐഐഐഐ

ONE WAY OR another, I would get back to him. A man who resisted questioning as stubbornly as Enrico might not be directly involved with the murder but it seemed reasonable to guess he had something to hide. And that something might be a clue.

If not a clue to murder, perhaps a clue to a reason for murder and so far we had no reason for this one. Motive, motive, motive. . . . Outside of Miss Thorne, who had a motive? And unless she knew about the will, she had none, or at least none that was as obvious as money.

Brentwood is not far from Santa Monica and I had an address there that would probably prove to be of only peripheral value, but the Lieutenant had made Miss Thorne my special assignment.

It was in an area of smaller homes, off Pico, a small house on the rear of a lot occupied by a slightly larger house. I walked along the common walk next to the larger house and came out into a world of flowers.

All the primaries were there, red, blue and yellow, and all the combinations of these—and it was only spring; the summer and fall flowers were not yet in bloom. At the side of the house, on a strip of lawn bordered by a low picket fence, an elderly couple were staining some outdoor redwood furniture. They looked up as I came along the steppingstones between the flower beds.

"Mr. and Mrs. Herbert Thorne?" I asked.

They nodded, and I looked at Mrs. Thorne. "I understand you were a good friend of Miss Milgrim's?"

She nodded. "Are you a reporter? Who told you that?"

"I'm not a reporter," I said. "Your daughter told me that."

"Oh," she said, and smiled. "Herbie, get the man a chair."

Her husband went around toward the back of the house. Mrs. Thorne sighed, and said, "We were both horribly shocked, of course. Mary Mae and I started together, at Biograph."

I stared at her and it came to me. "You're Blanche Arden," I said.

She smiled. "How sweet of you to remember. You're too young to remember me."

"I'll never forget you," I said. "I saw you in *Summer Thunder*. You were—unforgettable."

Her husband had brought a deck chair from the back yard. He set it down, and his wife said, "He remembers me, Herbie. That earns him a beer, doesn't it?" She looked at me. "You do drink, don't you?"

"Only beer," I said, "thank you." I sat in the deck chair and looked at the flowers. "Beautiful!"

Herbie went into the house and the former Blanche Arden sat on a redwood bench they hadn't started to stain. "Thank you. We love it here. We own the front house too, but we like it back here. We didn't save much, but we saved enough." She looked toward the house. "Herbie was a cameraman, and you know—he saved more than I did? He's a careful, wonderful man. I've been very lucky."

"Miss Milgrim saved her money, didn't she? She must have saved all of it?"

"She did better than that. She invested in real estate. We

used to laugh at her, to tease her about it. We thought she'd
gone insane when she paid seven hundred dollars for some
acreage way out on Sunset Boulevard." Mrs. Thorne shook
her head. "She sold it nine years ago for half a million."

"She must have been really loaded," I said, and looked
at the flowers.

The white-haired Herbie brought my beer and I thanked
him. I continued to look at the flowers as I repeated, "She
must have been really loaded. And yet, your daughter told
me last week that Miss Milgrim had to sell that house because
she needed the money desperately."

Mrs. Thorne smiled. Her husband looked grave.

"You know about it?" I guessed.

She nodded. "Mary Mae told me about it. About this
absurdly rich Texan who wouldn't submit an offer lower
than her asking price, this sentimental millionaire who refused to haggle with Mary Mae Milgrim." She sighed.
"When a man *asks* to be taken—"

Her husband said mildly, "Try to remember, Blanche,
that our visitor hasn't told us his name or the reason for his
visit."

Blanche looked blankly at her husband and wonderingly
at me. I was speechless for a moment.

Herbie filled the gap. "I happen to know who you are.
Played football with the Rams, didn't you? You're a private
eye, right?"

"Right as rain," I agreed. "Brock Callahan's the name.
Do you want your beer back?"

"Just want to know why you're here." Herbie said.

"To talk. To find out what I can about the lives, loves
and enemies of Mary Mae Milgrim. One of her fans is
paying me for this."

"A fan—?" Mrs. Thorne asked.

"My uncle," I said. "Homer Gallup, the man who bought
her house."

"Your *uncle—*?" Mrs. Thorne swallowed visibly. "Me and my big mouth." She looked at me beseechingly. "You're not going to tell him what I said, are you? I mean, what good would it do anybody?"

I said, "Not a word. I have a hunch Homer knows he was hornswoggled. Homer simply isn't a man who likes to quibble or haggle. He lives to enjoy life and keeps it that simple."

Mrs. Thorne looked questioningly at her husband and he, almost imperceptibly, nodded his head. He sat down next to her and she looked at me.

She took a breath and said, "We've been talking about what happened, Herbie and I. Mary Mae had a sharp tongue, you might have heard, and an artist's temperament. She was bound to have enemies." She paused, and again looked at her husband.

Again, the almost imperceptible nod.

She looked back at me. "But there's one man who has been a real—well I guess you'd call him a—a Svengali." She sighed. "He's certainly had an unholy influence on Mary Mae. Neither Herbie nor I could ever understand it. He's a mean and scheming man."

"Enrico Rivali," I guessed.

She nodded emphatically. "That's the man. You talked to him?"

"I've just come from his house. Are you thinking of him as the murderer?"

Mrs. Thorne didn't answer. Herbie said, "If we had to make a choice, he'd be our first."

"Why?" I asked.

There was a silence. Mrs. Thorne looked at her husband, as though waiting for him to word it.

Finally he said lamely, "Well, it's hard to say. When you come right down to it, neither of us knows much about what a murderer is like, but—'' He broke off, confused and irritated.

I smiled at Mrs. (Blanche Arden) Thorne. "But Enrico looks and acts like an old Biograph villain, is that it?"

She frowned, "It's not that—dumb, exactly. You know he's—not normal, don't you?"

I knew, but asked, "How?"

"He never married," she said primly.

"Neither did Mary Mae," I pointed out.

Herbie said evenly and clearly, "What Blanche means is that Rivali is a homo."

"And you think they murder more than other men?" I asked.

"I just mean he's not normal," Herbie said stubbornly. "And he's got a miserable temper and he's always playing the angles and he has no loyalty to anybody or anything. He's a *bastard!*"

"He could be all these things," I agreed. "But for murder, he'd need a motive. Can either of you come up with that?"

Blanche shook her head. Herbie said peevishly, "But that doesn't mean he wouldn't have a motive. A man as secretive as he's been since we've known him, he could have a dozen motives, and who'd know it?"

I nodded in silent agreement. And asked, "Do you know a man named George Parkas?"

They both nodded. Blanche said, "He used to play heavies. He was one of those—those freaks from Muscle Beach. I think he still hangs around there."

"Didn't he used to wrestle?" Herbie asked.

"He did. He's a friend of Rivali's, I guess. He was at his house, this morning anyway, and I had a feeling he lived there."

Herbie raised his eyebrows. "Birds of a feather—"

Mrs. Thorne made a face but said nothing.

I asked, "Your list of suspects begins and ends with Enrico, is that it?"

"He's the only one we could think of," Blanche admitted. "He's about all we have thought of, since it happened."

"But you'll do some more thinking, won't you?" I asked her. "There could easily be something in the background of Miss Milgrim that only her close friends know about. And it might help."

I thought the silence this time lasted a little longer than usual. And then Blanche Arden Thorne said, "Maybe we'll remember something. I'm sure we'll be thinking about nothing else for a while."

I thanked them for the beer and admired their flowers once more and went back to the hot flivver. I opened all the windows and got it under way quickly, to catch a breeze. It was turning into a hot afternoon.

Hot and fruitless; where next, semi-pro? That old sense of frustration came to me, that tiresome pattern of repetitive questioning in a circle of deceit. Around and around, getting this reaction, recording that lie, trying by stealth or arrogance to trigger a revealing straw in an erratic wind.

But where next now? Back to the office to think and sulk.

In the mail, there was a report from Lieutenant Remington and two bills. My answering service informed me there had been no calls in my absence. I opened the report.

It was a résumé of the information they had elicited from all the people at the party who had contributed anything in the form of a lead. There was very little here I didn't already know.

However, the last person to have been seen with Mary Mae *inside* the house had been Enrico Rivali. Half a dozen of the guests had testified to that.

He was the hub and the nub of it; that much seemed clear to me. He was the supreme schemer in a world of illusion. And a very hard nut to crack. As a suspect for murder, though, he looked weak. Where was the motive? What little I had learned indicated Mary Mae had been his sustenance; her death could be his suicide.

I opened a window and set a fan in front of it. I drank three glasses of water and went back to the report from Remington. Then I wheeled out my typewriter to start my own report for my files and for him.

I was about halfway through when somebody opened the door to my office.

The man who stood there was about six feet tall, fairly slim, and a little too well tailored. He had the easy poise and the candid gaze of the first-class confidence man.

"Mr. Brock Callahan?" he asked me quietly.

"At your service, sir." I stood up and indicated the chair on the other side of my desk.

"My name," he said, "is Everett Milgrim." He came over to sit down without offering me his hand.

"Oh—?" I said. "From—Florida?"

"Yes." He paused. "Currently, that is. You—have heard of me?"

"I heard Miss Milgrim had a brother in Florida. Are you he?"

"I'm Miss Milgrim's brother, yes. I'm not really *from* Florida. Recently, I've had reason to dabble in real estate down there, but I've always considered California my true home."

I nodded, smiled and said nothing.

"You," he said, "are representing a client named Homer Gallup in the investigation of my sister's death, I understand."

I nodded, leaned back and yawned.

His face stiffened slightly. "Am I boring you, Mr. Callahan?"

"No, Mr. Milgrim," I said blandly. "Carry on."

There was a pause. "I simply wondered what success

you've had in your investigation so far.''

"I've learned a few things, but nothing I could reveal to an outsider, Mr. Milgrim. I'm sure Lieutenant Remington, over at Beverly Hills Headquarters, would be co-operative, though. Perhaps you had better see him.''

Another pause while he seemed to be weighing me. "Mr. Callahan, we are both men of the world. And I have reason to know my sister's estate is enormous.'' He looked around my office casually. "And you don't appear to be the—wealthiest man in this wealthy man's town.''

"I guess I'm not,'' I agreed. "Get to the meat, Everett.''

He smiled. "That's blunt enough. I'm the closest relative. I'm the *only* close relative. And I can use an ally.''

"If it's crooked,'' I told him, "I'm not interested. If it's business, you know I already have a client in this case.''

"You can always quit a client,'' he said, "if you find a better one, can't you?''

I shook my head. "Mr. Milgrim, weren't you formerly in business in this town?''

He nodded. "Some years back. I had a brokerage office. Dealt mostly in over-the-counter stocks.''

I frowned. "If I remember right, the SEC issued a cease-and-desist. But I forget if they called your place a bucket shop or a boiler room.''

For a transient moment, his poise was gone. But it had returned before he spoke. "I'll say it again—you're a blunt man.''

"Thank you. Was that why you came here instead of going to Lieutenant Remington? Because Remington might remember you?''

He didn't answer. His eyes glazed over and his face was without expression.

"Whom did you want me to frame?'' I asked him quietly.

"I thought I could help you,'' he said sadly. "I thought I could help you professionally and financially. But you seem to have developed an aversion either to me or to the prospects of a handsome and perfectly legitimate profit. I guess I came to the wrong man, didn't I?''

"It's possible. It's also possible that you came at the wrong time. I heard that you had been out of touch with your sister for twenty years. And now, like a homing vulture, you travel across the country to share in the profits of the killing. I think you'd better go."

He stood up. ''You're more than blunt. You're insulting. You're also extremely stupid, aren't you?''

"I'm also big," I added. "Start running, Milgrim. Go!"

His glance swept my neat little pine-paneled office contemptuously, rested briefly on me, and then he turned and went out.

I had handled it badly. Perhaps he knew something and I had alienated him without reason. He wasn't lost, however. I had a feeling I'd be seeing him again.

I finished the report and made out an envelope addressed to Lieutenant Remington. I put a carbon of the report in the envelope, sealed it, stamped it, and went down to my flivver. It was almost five o'clock.

At the liquor store, half a block up the street, I picked up a fifth of the most expensive Scotch in the place.

EIGHT

IT WAS A four-unit, weathered stucco building on Kenmore in Hollywood. The apartment of the distinguished and immortal John Davenport, former idol of millions, was a no-bedroom unit in the rear.

He stood in the doorway and looked at me doubtfully. "Is the liquor a gift or did you intend to buy my autograph with it?"

"It's a gift," I said. "Though I'm digging into a personal history."

"I'm not a historian," he said.

I shrugged.

He studied me and then looked down at the bottle in my hand. "Would you let me see the label, please?"

I held it up. He nodded and said, "Come on in."

The furniture wasn't much. A studio couch, an old wooden card table on which he obviously ate, two worn, upholstered easy chairs and a coffee table made from a piano bench. The walls were covered with photographs, a number of them stills from his pictures, the others autographed to him from the big names of yesterday.

I stood next to a picture of Mary Mae Milgrim as he opened the Scotch. On it, she had scrawled, "To stubborn and gifted John Davenport."

"Neat," he asked me, "or with water?"

"I don't drink the hard stuff," I said. "I'll take a beer if you've got it."

He made a face. "I don't drink the soft stuff. I could make you some coffee."

"No, thanks. Do you know Mrs. Herbie Thorne?"

He shook his head. He lifted a shot of Scotch to the light, admired it and downed it. Then he frowned. "Wait—do you mean Blanche Arden?"

"That's right."

"Wonderful woman," he said. "Kind and sweet and generous. Is she still around?"

"She married a cameraman. She's living in Santa Monica." I sat in one of the upholstered chairs.

He sat on the piano bench-coffee table, the bottle beside him. "Blanche Arden—wonderful girl. A minimum of talent but a maximum of fun. Oh, there were a million of those and I loved every one of them."

"She's Joyce Thorne's mother," I explained. "Joyce was Miss Milgrim's secretary."

"Oh," he said. "Oh, yes." He poured another drink.

"Why did Miss Milgrim call you stubborn?" I asked.

He glanced at the picture and smiled. "Because I was. I was probably the only name she couldn't inveigle into a supporting role." He looked thoughtfully at the glass in his hand. "You know, Mary Mae was all right. If it hadn't been for Rivali, I think Mary Mae could have turned out a first-class person."

"You don't think she did?"

He looked at me. "As an actress or a person?"

"Either and both."

"Well," he said slowly, "there wasn't any need for her to become an actress; she was a star. As a person, I think Rivali's influence was overwhelming. She wound up as fraudulent and greedy as her—her Svengali."

That was the second time today poor Enrico had been

called that. I said, "Blanche Arden doesn't think much of Rivali either. As a matter of fact, it's hard to find anyone with a good word for the man."

"Ask him," Davenport said dryly. "He's got plenty of them." He shook his head. "Blanche Arden. She lived in the shadow of Mary Mae. And that was the only way to remain a friend of Mary's, to live in her shadow." He smiled at me. "Perhaps I wouldn't be living here if I had, huh?"

"Who knows?" I said. "Most of us are what we have to be." I looked around at all the pictures. "Do you regret being what you were?"

"Not for a second." He corked the bottle, stood up and went over to put it on the kitchen drainboard. He drank a glass of water in there and came back through the archway to sit on the bench again.

"Rivali," I said. "He's been called a schemer and a crook, a Svengali and a no-talent bum. But can you see him as a murderer?"

John Davenport said steadily. "I can see him as absolutely *anything* he has to be to protect his interest or advance his nefarious career."

"I heard a rumor that he and Mary Mae were once married. Anything to it?"

"Nothing," John Davenport said. "Rivali started the rumor, for reasons too complex for my simple and honorable mind. That bastard maintained his own position by keeping everybody else off balance, but it's a technique too complicated for the ordinary mentality. I could never understand it and I certainly couldn't explain it. He never went to jail, I'll admit, but in these last few years his position has been more desperate. And perhaps that called for more desperate measures."

"How about this George Parkas? I had a feeling he lives with Rivali."

Davenport smiled cynically. "He's been faithful to George for a number of years, now. It wasn't always thus."

"Fickle, was he?"

Davenport nodded. "I suppose that facet of his personality could have landed him in jail. But if all the homos in this town were put behind bars, there wouldn't be room for anything else."

"Wasn't there ever a time when Enrico was interested in girls?"

Davenport shrugged. "Perhaps, as a youth, in Italy. . . . Never, so long as I knew him." He looked longingly toward the bottle on the drainboard in the kitchen.

"Don't let me stop you," I said.

"No," he said. "No, not any more until I've eaten. You know, it was never a problem with me, until the last few months, since I've started to get some work again, in TV. Why should something I've enjoyed all my life now suddenly turn into a crutch?"

"You're not young," I said. "And with a new career starting, you might feel insecure. And before this you had an agent to act as a buffer between you and reality."

"That he was," Davenport admitted. "A buffer between me and all the idiots in this idiotic business. And a wall between me and steady meals. I guess the son of a bitch did serve a purpose, though, didn't he?"

"The maintenance of an ego," I said, "is a difficult and thankless profession."

He looked at me doubtfully. "You think I'm an ego?"

"Any successful artist has to be," I argued. I indicated the pictures on the walls. "Some of those people were at the party, weren't they?"

"A number of them. I doubt if there's a murderer in a carload of them, though."

"Murder is a state of mind," I said. "There must have been a few enemies in the gang. There must have been some feuds you know about."

"A thousand," he agreed. "But how many of them were current, I couldn't know. One thing about Hollywood feuds, most of them are highly impermanent. And quite a few of them, of course, exist only in the minds of the publicity men who spawn them and the gullible fans who read that garbage. I can't honestly think of a single person at that party who hated Mary Mae enough to do what was done. She wasn't— indiscriminately malicious, you know. She made the right enemies and none of the important ones would be invited to her party."

Perhaps, I thought, *Miss Thorne would invite the important ones. If she knew she was to inherit all that money . . . .*

"What are you thinking?" John Davenport asked.

"Something I'm not free to voice." I stood up. "Well, good luck with your new career."

"Thank you," he said. He looked uncomfortable for a moment. "I suppose Mr. Gallup won't be financing any picture, now."

"I doubt it."

He cleared his throat. "In the event you see him, you might mention that I have a rather—interesting part in 'Playhouse 90' Thursday night. It could—lead somewhere."

"I'll be sure to tell him," I promised. "He's a great fan of yours."

He had been a star in a medium run by fools and was now trying to get a new start in a medium run by thieves. Some life. And still young men aspired to be actors.

It was six o'clock and most of the going-home traffic was already home. To my right, now, were the stone pillars that flanked the driveway leading to Homer's horror.

A car coming from the other direction had stopped, its signal flashing, waiting to turn into the driveway. It was a Merc with Florida plates, and though I didn't get a clear look at the driver, what I saw of him convinced me it was Everett Milgrim.

I had an impulse to go back but a stonger impulse to feed

my growling stomach. I drove on, toward Carl's Steak House.

Carl's steaks were nothing special but he had Einlicher and it was a benediction I owed myself after the frustrating day. I sipped and thought of Everett Milgrim.

Homer and Aunt Sheila wouldn't be moving in for another week. Which meant that Everett had gone there to see either Joyce Thorne or Raymond Yoshida. I had to assume it was Miss Thorne.

And from there I had a choice of two assumptions. Everett had gone to see her one of two ways—invited or uninvited.

Miss Thorne, despite her air of cool competence, was on the lamb side of my ledger and I had a pathological compulsion to always protect the lambs. Against the lions or the wolves or even a fox like Mary Mae's no-good brother, Everett.

So two Einlichers and one T-bone later, I was again chugging down Sunset, the flivver complaining of these extra hours of labor. It was dark now, and a thin rind of moon looked compassionately down from a star-speckled sky. It was a sumptuous, silky night, an M-G-M epic type of night, the kind of nights we used to have before the corn-belt invasion.

I turned off Sunset into an even older world, between the stone pillars, and the rasp of gravel under my retreaded tires whispered sadly, longing for the feel of buggy wheels.

It seemed cooler suddenly, the stars hidden by the poplars overhead, the thin moon lost behind the towering castle at the end of the road. There was a dim light in the apartment over the garage and a brighter light showing in Miss Thorne's cottage.

There was no sign of the Florida Mercury. I parked just beyond the drawbridge, in the shadow of an immense bird of paradise tree, and walked quietly back toward the garages. I wanted to see the parking area on the far side.

There was no Merc here either. From overhead came the

sound of music, oriental music, dissonant, with a complex rhythm, and a shadow moved behind the lighted window above. I walked carefully back toward the cottage.

The door chime was audible from where I stood. In a few seconds, a voice said, "Who is it?"

"Brock Callahan, Miss Thorne."

A pause and, "Just a minute, please."

Footsteps, going and coming, and when she finally opened the door, she was wearing a robe.

"I'm sorry," I said. "Were you about to retire?"

She shook her head. "I was about to change. I intended to go out for dinner, but I don't think I will. Come in."

I came into the gabled living room. All the drapes were drawn except one at the far end of the room.

"Sit down," she said, and I sat on a soft, long sofa upholstered in a flowered, nubby fabric.

"Drink?" she asked.

I shook my head and wondered at the change in her. She hadn't been this cordial this morning. I said, "I was driving past here on my way to dinner when I saw a car turn in. I have reason to think the driver was Everett Milgrim. Did he come to see you?"

Her blue eyes grew wide and she said quietly. "No, he didn't. Was it a cream-colored car with a Florida license?"

"That's right."

"He went to see Raymond," she said. "Mr. Yoshida. He spent almost an hour there. Why would he do that?"

"I don't know. He's—not the most solid citizen in the world, this Milgrim, you know."

"I know," she said softly. "I know. I—need a drink." She turned and went toward the dining L, out of my range of vision.

A phone rang and she must have picked it up in there, because I heard her say, "I've decided to stay home." Pause. "No, not tonight." Pause. "Do that." Pause. "Please, don't be a pest. Good night." The clack of the phone being replaced on its cradle.

She came back into the room, a long glass in her hand, an amber liquid, loaded with ice cubes.

"Two-bit producers," she said. She lifted the glass. "Phooey!" She drank.

"They're used to better treatment in this town," I said. "You never know when one of them might connect."

"This one never will. He never gets out of the bedroom long enough to function. Are you sure you don't want a drink, Mr. Callahan?"

"I rarely drink," I said. "Perhaps, later."

She sat in the chintzy, upholstered chair and the robe fell away from her leg. The ivory of her skin glowed in the light from the far end of the room. An indoor girl, a hot-house flower. . . .

"I treated you badly this morning, didn't I?" she asked.

I shrugged. "I'm used to it. Are you frightened tonight?"

She stared, then nodded. "Perceptive, aren't you? I suppose that's a requirement of your—profession. It is a profession, isn't it?"

"It depends on who's running it, I guess, Miss Thorne. To some it's a trade and to others a racket. I try to stay professional, but it isn't always easy. Tell me, how close were your mother and Miss Milgrim?"

She said slowly, "I think my mother was as close to Mary Mae as any person ever was. People—confided in my mother."

"What's her background—Mary Mae's, I mean?"

Joyce Thorne paused, sipping her drink thoughtfully. "I suppose it sounds disloyal, but I'd call it a pseudo-Southern, small-town gentility. She played the—the vulnerable daughter and took some satisfaction, I'm sure, in her brother's role of the spoiled son."

"Pseudo-Southern—? You mean she wasn't from the South?"

"Northern Indiana. Is that the real South?"

"I suppose not. It's a Big Ten state and I've always considered that the Middle West, but I'm thinking athletically, I guess." My glance moved to the ivory calf and returned to her blue eyes. "She really didn't hate her brother then?"

She frowned. "I'm no psychiatrist. But I think she was glad she had a relative to hate. I had a feeling she would have felt worse without a worthless relative. Does that make sense?"

"I don't know. Would it be like a—a martyr complex?"

She shook her head. Then she smiled. "Perhaps it made her feel more authentically Southern, having a worthless brother. Her ideas of authenticity came from a wide background of reading among the second-rate female historical novelists."

This cool dissecting of a shallow personality was different from her morning's declaration of love for Mary Mae. I couldn't think of anything to say.

"I'm shocking you," she said.

"Ah—no."

"I loved her. But that wouldn't make me blind. She was kind to me and never once made me feel inferior in any way. I—loved her and always will."

"And why are you frightened tonight?" I asked.

She stared at the floor. "That—castle. Those shadows. And my God, it—happened last night, didn't it? I'm not steel."

A light flashed across the one undraped window and brought both our heads around that way. It was a headlight from Sunset Boulevard that had reflected off the windshield of my car out in the courtyard.

Joyce Thorne expelled her breath slowly. "Is that your car out there?"

"Yes. Didn't you see me drive up?"

"I must have been in the bathroom." She stood up and went over to pull the unpulled drape. Her silk robe swished softly as she walked.

"I need another drink," she said, and went into the dining L again.

My God, it happened last night, didn't it. . . . She was so right. I had assumed Everett Milgrim had flown out as soon as he was notified. I had assumed that in my office. But he was here with his car. He hadn't driven out here in that length of time; he must have been in town before Mary Mae was killed.

Joyce Thorne came back with a new drink and I asked her, "Was there some kind of crisis looming in the Milgrim family?"

"No. Not to my knowledge." She sat in the chintzy chair again and the robe slid higher this time. "Why?"

"I wondered why her brother was in town. Do you know how long he's been in town?"

She shook her head.

"This morning you told me he'd been notified. Who notified him?"

"Miss Milgrim's attorney. A man named McAllister; I forget the name of the firm. They're on Beverly Drive."

I put the name down, the efficient investigator, trying not to think of that lustrous thigh now visible.

She said, "You went to visit my folks this morning, didn't you?"

"This afternoon," I admitted. "I thought your mother could give me some revealing information on Miss Milgrim. Your mother's quite a girl."

She nodded and smiled.

"Still frightened?" I asked her.

She nodded again. "That Yoshida—Is it bigotry to be afraid of him?"

"Partially, I suppose. Has he ever given you reason to be afraid of him?"

"N-no. He has a rather superior and enigmatic smile and I never thought he had the—humility you'd expect from a gardener, but he's certainly never been insolent."

I said nothing. And for seconds, she said nothing. The silence seemed to make her nervous; she pulled the robe over her leg and glanced briefly at the window at the far end of the room. She picked at some lint on the robe.

"Well," I said, "I'd better be going."

She looked up quickly. "Not yet—You don't *have* to go right now, do you?"

"Not if you're still frightened. Would you feel better if I slept here tonight?"

Some color in the ivory cheeks and her chin lifted.

"I'm a well-trained domestic animal," I assured her, "and come only when called. You needn't fear me."

"What would people say?" she asked softly.

"What people? Yoshida?"

She nodded.

"He'd gossip, probably," I agreed. "Why don't you go to a hotel for the night?"

"No. I—wish you'd have a drink."

I didn't know where we were heading, but it looked like an interesting road. "Okay," I said. "Bourbon and water, light on the bourbon." I was getting to be a real soak.

So we sat and talked, but not about the murder. She told me about her five years at UCLA and I gave her the highlights of my stellar career at Stanford and with the Rams. We got to be friends, kind of.

Don't get me wrong; no woman can buy me with her body. But only a prude would discourage them from trying.

NINE

A LADY OF decorum in the drawing room, a cool, intelligent and articulate beauty, this Joyce Arden Thorne, gracious hostess, efficient secretary. A woman, you would guess, with her emotions under proper discipline and a not-too-obvious eye for the main chance.

In the bedroom, she was savage, withdrawing, squirming away, staging it as though it were rape, with many hoarse protestations followed by even more furious demands and soaring co-operation. In the drawing room, adjusted; horizontally, a complex savage.

Spent, scratched, one ear bitten, in the servants' cottage, quiescent and bewildered, I lay next to the marble and pink body.

"Don't get any ideas," she said quickly.

"I haven't the strength for an idea. What ideas shouldn't I get?"

"Any romantic notions—or hopes. This was—medical."

I said nothing.

"A girl can stay bottled up just so long. You arrived at a fortunate moment."

"For whom? For you or for me?"

Silence from her and then a small, smothered laugh. "I deserved that, I guess. I'm tired. Are you tired?"

"I'm tired. I'll find another bed. If you have any further

demands, ring for me." I took a blanket along and went
out to the soft, long couch in the living room.

There, as I settled down, I thought of the two-bit producer
and wondered if I had robbed him of the sustenance of all
two-bit producers. I had other hobbies but producers were
inclined to be single-minded about their recreational pur-
suits.

Well, it was too late to help him now; I stretched and
yawned and tried not to think of Jan. That was always the
hardest part, trying not to think of Jan. I am monogamous
by instinct, but Jan is emotionally erratic, with long barren
stretches for which I must maintain outside sources.

Women. . . . The poor bedeviled devils. . . . I fell asleep
feeling sorry for the producer.

In the morning, I woke early. From far below, on Sunset,
a siren wailed and it might have been that which had wakened
me. There was no sound in the house.

The blanket was stifling me, the pillow I'd borrowed
from her bed was wet with perspiration. She had probably
forgotten to turn down the thermostat last night. I rose and
went to the bathroom.

I found a razor and shaved. I showered and dressed and
went out to the living room again. Still no sound from her
and an unreasonable nervousness moved through me and I
went to her open bedroom to check.

She was lying on her bed, uncovered, unclothed, as naked
as I had left her last night. She had a beautifully shaped
body and at the moment it was as quiet as statuary. I stared,
searching for a sign of her breathing.

She opened her eyes and said, *"Voyeur?* Close the door,
please, from the other side of it."

I closed the door and went to the kitchen. I drank two
glasses of milk and rummaged for some eggs and bacon.
There were both and I took them out and opened some more
cabinet doors until I found the toaster and the bread box.

I heard the water running in the bathroom as I was taking the butter out of the refrigerator. I went into the living room with yesterday's afternoon paper.

She came in there about five minutes later to ask, "Does all that preparation in the kitchen mean you planned to have breakfast here?"

"If it's all right with you," I answered. "I hate those drugstore lunch-counter breakfasts."

She sighed. "I hope you won't think it's unduly maidenly of me, but I've never faced a man over a breakfast table in my own place before."

"Okay," I said, "I'll go."

"No. Stay. I suppose it's good training for marriage."

It was a mistake. She was strained and embarrassed, as though I had uncovered a major character defect in her.

We were on our coffee when her door chime sounded. She looked doubtfully at me and then at the clock above the sink. It was only eight o'clock.

A pause, and then she rose and went to the door.

I could hear our visitor's voice from where I sat. It was Homer. He said, "We wanted to look at the house, but we forgot to bring a key. We thought you might have one."

We, we, we. . . . Who was "we"? He and Aunt Shelia? Or he and Aunt Shelia *and Jan?* Jan would recognize my car. And then I realized Homer would too. He had recognized it on the parking lot.

Joyce said, "I have a key. Wait; I'll get it."

I had an impulse to go out to talk with him, but an even stronger impulse to sit where I was sitting.

Joyce brought the key and Homer thanked her. And then added, "By the way, is that Mr. Callahan's car in the court?"

I started to get up—and Joyce said, "I think so. He was measuring the moat a little while ago, over there near the drawbridge. He might be talking with Mr. Yoshida. He spent a lot of time with him yesterday."

Homer thanked her again and I heard the door close.

Joyce came back to the kitchen, her color high, her eyes avoiding mine. She walked right over to a drawer and took out a small, ten-foot steel measuring tape.

She said hoarsely, "Mr. and Mrs. Gallup are out there. *And Miss Bonnet!*" She set the tape on the kitchen table noisily. "I hope you overheard my explanation."

"I did," I said. "I—uh—"

She picked the tape up again and slapped it into my hand. She pointed. "The back door. Right there!"

It was kind of undignified, I thought. I hadn't been the aggressor last night. A guilty participant, yes, but most of it had been *her* idea.

I said, "Good morning," stiffly and went out the back door.

From the rear of the castle, I heard the racket of a power mower, and I worked that way, trying to keep as much shrubbery as possible between me and any views from the castle.

Raymond Yoshida looked up as I came into the clearing where he was cutting a strip of dichondrae. Joyce was right about him. His smile was superior and enigmatic.

"Good morning, Mr. Callahan," he said politely. He slowed the engine to a quieter tone. "Sleep well?"

I stared at him. He smiled at me.

"I never got to bed," I told him. "On the important cases, I often work right through, seventy-two, often ninety-six hours. I'm very strong and don't need sleep."

I smiled at him. He stared at me.

"You had a visitor yesterday," I said quietly. "A Mr. Everett Milgrim."

"Yes." Toneless voice, blank stare.

"Be careful of him," I warned. "If you want the word on him, they have it at Beverly Hills Police Headquarters. He'd be the wrong man for you to do any business with."

"Business?" he asked dully. "I'm not going into any business."

"I hope not," I said. "We wouldn't want *my uncle* to lose a first-class gardener, would we?"

He expelled his breath. "I don't understand you, Mr. Callahan."

"Mr. Milgrim stayed a long time. What did you talk about?"

"About his sister. He wanted to know if she had been happy. He maybe thinks she committed suicide. And then he wanted to know if she had been seeing much of Mr. Rivali and how they were getting along."

"And you told him about the fight you overheard between her and Rivali?"

He shook his head emphatically. "No. Never. I said Mr. Rivali was here often and I didn't know how they got along."

"And then—?"

"And then he asked about Miss Thorne and how they got along."

"And you told him—?"

"I told him I didn't know."

"He had no authority, Raymond, to ask you any questions."

"Maybe not. He didn't ask them like a—a policeman. And he's Miss Milgrim's brother, isn't he? I couldn't be rude, could I?"

"No. But next time he asks any questions, you explain that Lieutenant Remington, down at Headquarters, doesn't want you to discuss Miss Milgrim with anyone."

A thoughtful pause, and then, "Lieutenant Remington can't keep me from talking about anything I want to. Doing, he can stop. But not talking."

"You're right," I agreed. "I wasn't giving you an order; I was giving you an excuse for avoiding Everett Milgrim. I thought I was doing you a favor."

He said nothing, staring at me.

And then he looked past me and I turned to see what he was looking at, and it was my Jan, heading our way, her face stormy.

I nodded a goodbye to Yoshida and went over to meet Jan. I didn't want her to start complaining where anyone could hear us.

"Well—!" she said for a starter. "And where were you last night?"

"Why?" I asked. "We didn't have a date, did we?"

"I called you at one o'clock and you weren't home. And where did you have breakfast?"

"At one o'clock," I said, "I was on my way back from Bakersfield. Breakfast I ate at Marge and Joe's Delightful Diner on Olympic Boulevard. What in the hell difference does it make where I had breakfast?"

"You liar," she said. "You lying, rotten tomcat."

"Easy, now," I said. "Where were you last night, so drunk that you'd call me at one o'clock?"

"Never mind where I was. Don't you think I can see the dew all over your car, there in the court? Brock Callahan, don't you ever talk to me again!" She went past me, toward Yoshida.

She wasn't sure, not completely. Or why would she be going over to question Yoshida? I gave her my proud back and went toward the house.

Homer and my aunt were in the ballroom, studying the high windows.

"We could take that wall out and put in sliding glass," my aunt was explaining. "Turn this into the living room and the living room into a playroom and—" She turned, saw me, and sniffed.

"Good morning, Brock, old buddy," Homer said. "Been up early, measuring the moat, I see."

"Right," I said. "Some moat!"

"Some story," my Aunt Sheila said scornfully. "Men. Miserable, stinking men—"

"Take it easy," Homer soothed her. And to me, as warning. "We called you, about one o'clock last night, Brock. Where were you?"

"Coming back from Bakersfield," I said.

"Oh," Homer said. "You decided to go see Thompson, after all, then?"

My Homer! My discerning, compassionate, quick-thinking, wonderfully fraudulent uncle. . . .

"Yup," I said. "And you were right about him. He just hasn't the kind of make-up murder requires."

"No kidding," Aunt Sheila said. "How is he on lying?"

I looked bewildered, Homer shrugged and asked mildly. "What did you plan to do with that wall, again, Sheila?"

"Open it up," she said. "Put in a whole bank of sliding glass."

"That would cost money," Homer said thoughtfully. "And I'm sure you wouldn't expect a miserable, stinking man to go digging down into his wallet just—"

"Stop!" she said fiercely. "Have you any kind of damned, stupid, Texas idea that you can *buy me,* Homer Gallup?"

He said in dignified shock, "Buy you—? You love me; I don't have to buy you, darling. You'd love me if I didn't have a dime."

She looked at him suspiciously, and then at me. She said, "You two found each other, didn't you?" And to me: "Where's Jan?"

"Last I saw of her she was outside, talking to the gardener."

Sheila went out and Homer looked at me. "You damned fool," he said.

I said nothing.

"Your car sitting there, in the shade, full of last night's

dew. I thought Jan was going to force her way into that cottage.''

"She must learn not to judge by appearances," I said. "Everett Milgrim came to see Yoshida yesterday. They talked for a long time. Miss Thorne's parents have only one suspect, Enrico Rivali. Outside of that, I haven't learned much, Homer."

"Well," he said, "you're having fun, anyway. You can't work all the time."

"I'll quit now," I said, "if you think you're not getting your money's worth."

He frowned. "Sensitive? Did I say something wrong?"

"I'm sorry," I said. "I feel guilty. I'm a bum."

"You sure as hell are," he agreed. "You'd better get out of here before Jan comes back. And you'd better include in your report to me a few paragraphs about that trip to Bakersfield. I'll leave it around where your aunt can find it. Now, beat it; I hear 'em coming."

I got out before they came in. I went home and put on a clean shirt and pair of socks and went back to the office.

There was a check in the mail. And my answering service informed me that Enrico Rivali had phoned but left no message except that he would phone again. I went to work on the report for yesterday and this morning, putting in the counterfeit Bakersfield trip.

Then I phoned Enrico Rivali, but there was no answer. I phoned the offices of Darrow, Weldon and Lutz and Mr. Wallace Darrow was available. I asked him if he would be there for a while.

He was going out for breakfast, he said. If I wanted to see him, he could drop in at my office.

While I waited, I phoned Remington and told him about Milgrim's visit yesterday.

"I've just finished reading your report on that," he said. "Where is he staying?"

"I don't know. I can find out. But he didn't come from Florida *after* Miss Milgrim died. Because he's here with his car. I mean, of course, he didn't *start* for here after she died."

"I see. He's got quite a record in this town. We can pick him up on suspicion of practically anything."

"You going to crowd him a little, Lieutenant?"

"We don't normally harass citizens in this town," he informed me stiffly. "But Mr. Milgrim isn't exactly a normal citizen."

"Right," I soothed him. "Raymond Yoshida, that gardener of Miss Milgrim's, might have Everett's address. They had a long talk together yesterday, in Raymond's apartment over the garage there."

"Thanks," he said. "We'll look into that."

He had actually thanked me. I hung up, glowing.

I was nostalgically fingering my bitten ear when Wallace Darrow walked into the office.

"Well," he asked in his breezy way, "what's on your mind, Brock?"

"Murder," I said. "Sit down, Mr. Darrow."

"My friends call me Wallace," he said.

"That's logical," I admitted. "Mr. Darrow, I've been looking back on the sale of that Milgrim house to Mr. Gallup and certain aspects of the deal shock me a little."

He looked at me coolly. "Be careful, now. I have an umblemished reputation and I resent any slurs."

"If you have an unblemished reputation," I told him candidly, "you're in the wrong business. Or you're broke. I don't think you are. I happen to know about the Academy Award performance you and Miss Bonnet put on for the one-person audience composed of my beloved aunt."

He smiled. "Oh, that—It was Mr. Gallup's idea and Mr. Gallup was my client."

"That makes it all right?"

He shrugged.

"And," I went on, "my aunt has learned that house was in escrow a few months back at a purchase price of eighty-five thousand dollars."

He said evenly, "You were there when I suggested to Mr. Gallup that he offer a lower price. You heard his answer."

"True enough. Would you mind telling me why that other escrow fell through?"

"I don't have to, but I will. The buyer was firm on insisting on getting the mineral rights. Miss Milgrim was equally adamant about relinquishing them." He spread his hands. "No deal."

"And who suggested that Miss Thorne phone me with the sob story about Miss Milgrim's great poverty before Homer Gallup took the bait?"

"I didn't know Miss Thorne ever phoned you," he said quietly.

"In this deal, did Homer insist on the mineral rights?"

He nodded, and added, "At my suggestion. At that price, I was trying to get him as much as I could."

I was quiet for a few seconds. And then I asked, "You're a good friend of Miss Thorne's, aren't you?"

He smiled. "I guess. Aren't you?"

"What did you mean by that?"

His chin lifted. "You read it any damned way you want to. You're not a police officer, Callahan, and I resent the insolent implications of your questioning."

"I'm working very closely with the police," I told him. "At *their* suggestion."

"I'll bet," he said.

"I reported to Lieutenant Remington just before you came in," I went on. "I can phone him back if you'd like to confirm my position."

"Don't bother," he said. "I know all about you and how

you work. I don't mind adding that I had a date with Miss Thorne last night for dinner, a date she didn't keep. I dropped over there and saw why."

"Why didn't you knock, if you had a date?"

"You were there when I phoned her. You heard her break the date."

She had lied . . . . This was the alleged two-bit producer. Why had she lied?

Darrow said calmly, "I wasn't completely honest with your aunt about the sale of the Milgrim place. Do you want me to be just as dishonest with Miss Bonnet? You kill me, you and your cheap talk about ethics."

I stared at him. "You do get around, don't you?"

He stood up. "I try not to atrophy." He took a breath. "Or panic. Do you think your size frightens me?"

I had to admire him. "You bastard," I said. "I underestimated you. Maybe my size doesn't frighten you, but your mind scares the hell out of me."

"Let's keep it that way," he said, and turned to go.

As Enrico Rivali entered. They were both motionless for a moment, and I was sure there was animosity in both their glances. Then Wallace said, "Well, hello."

And Rivali said, "Hanky pank, eh? You two are planning, maybe, to get deeper into the pocket of Mr. Gallup?"

"Nothing of the kind," Wallace said airily. "Callahan called me in to get the low-down on you, Enrico. And I've just finished giving it to him."

He waved, and went past Rivali through the doorway. Rivali muttered something in what sounded like Italian and came over to sit in the chair Darrow had just vacated.

He stared at me sullenly. "A real tricky son of a bitch, that Darrow."

I smiled, but only inwardly. The pot was describing the kettle. I asked, "Why are you here, Mr. Rivali? Have an attack of conscience?"

"Maybe, maybe. You think I couldn't?"

I smiled outwardly. "Why not?"

He gestured. "I was rude and George was—inexcusable. You came at a bad time with impertinent questions. But I apologize."

"And George?" I asked. "I hope I didn't injure him seriously."

"No. He is—not as repentant as I am. He is less well adjusted. But a good friend of mine and I apologize for him." He fidgeted in his chair. "What did that Wallace tell you about me?"

"Nothing. He was teasing you when he left. Your name was never mentioned in our conversation."

He stared at me skeptically.

"I swear it, Enrico. Did you come here only to apologize?"

"No." He paused. "Mary Mae's brother is in town."

"I know it. He came to see me."

Enrico looked startled. "You—? Why?"

"I never really found out. It sounded crooked and I told him to beat it."

"Mary Mae hated him," Rivali said musingly, "but who else did she have? He's probably the heir, don't you think?"

I smiled and said nothing.

"Well—?" he said irritatedly.

"Enrico," I asked him, "did you come here to tell me something or to pump me?"

The dark eyes flashed and the sallow face tightened. "To warn you, about this Milgrim. If he isn't the heir, God help the heir."

"You think he's that rough? Con men usually don't play it heavy. They're too smart for that."

"He's more than talk, that man. He's—evil."

"Have you talked with him?"

A pause, and then Enrico nodded.

"Did he—proposition you?"

"He tried to question me about the will. He said if anybody would know about the will, I would. I was her closest friend. He said her lawyers wouldn't tell him anything. Why are they so secretive?"

I shrugged. "They don't confide in me."

"But the police do," he persisted.

"Occasionally," I admitted. "Was that all you had to tell me, that Everett Milgrim was evil?"

He nodded.

"You don't want to tell me why you threatened Miss Milgrim?"

"I didn't. Whoever told you that lied."

"All right. Thanks for the information. And now, if you don't mind, I have to get back to work."

He muttered something in Italian, stood up and glared at me for a few seconds. Then he went out, still muttering.

It amazed me that he had come to power while the Hungarians reigned. He was about as subtle as a burlesque comedian.

TEN

Now, IF YOU don't mind, I have to get back to work . . . .

A cliché, used for dismissal. Back to work where? Enrico still looked like the hub of this wheel, but he was undoubtedly a man who had kept his tracks well covered. And murder needs a motive.

He had called Milgrim evil, but evil means different things to different people. To some, I had been evil last night. Others draw the line at murder but not at robbing widows. Murder stories pass the censor easily, but sex runs into trouble spasmodically. Is murder less evil than adultery? Only in America, this country of moral bewilderment.

I left my car on the parking lot and, full of confused musings, walked over to Headquarters. I found Sergeant Gnup and a uniformed man talking in a small room near Remington's office.

Gnup looked at me hopefully, but I shook my head.

"We've got a lead on the coniine—*maybe*," he said. "I'm checking it out after lunch."

"A lead to whom?"

"Nobody, yet," he said. "A source, with possible Mafia tie-up."

I thought of Rivali, but said nothing.

"The standard American hoodlum doesn't go in much

for poison," Gnup went on, "but who in hell is standard in this mess?"

"And who's a hoodlum?" I added. "Did Lieutenant Remington tell you about Everett Milgrim being in town?"

"Yup." Gnup grinned. "We'll keep 'im off balance. We put Reuter on it."

Reuter, too, had once played professional football. With the Bears. I said, "Nothing you can hold him on, though?"

Gnup shook his head. "He was too slippery for that. A real operator." He gave the uniformed man some papers and the man went out. He looked at me and sighed. "Do you think we're on this side of the law only because we're dumb?"

"It could be. We're nowhere, aren't we?"

"Not if this lead to the poison pans out. We're always nowhere just before the light."

It was time for lunch. And though I had had a full breakfast, I was ready to eat.

At the drugstore, my fan was not in sight. He probably had a day off. A dark, stocky girl took my order stoically; I missed my fan.

There was a copy of yesterday's paper on the counter; I picked it up and leafed through the story I'd already read, glanced again at the pictures.

For a fractional moment, a flash of awareness flared in me and then died. Something in the pictures had triggered my investigating prescience for that slice of a second—and then vanished without identifying itself. I thought, thought and thought while I stared at the pictures, but nothing came.

Three stools closer to the front door, my beloved was now seating herself. Next to her, my Aunt Sheila was also taking a stool.

"Hey, girls!" I called. "Down here." I pointed to the empty stools to the right of me.

Both of them turned their heads my way but on neither

face was there any sign of recognition. I was getting the freeze.

I looked back at the pictures in the paper and then folded the paper and put it into my jacket pocket.

The beef stew was only fair, despite the new cook. The coffee was fresh and flavorful. I had two cups of that while I searched my mind for the vagrant lead that had almost come to life.

Up the counter, my friend and my relative ignored me. Undoubtedly, they were discusssing how to make a *moderne* house out of the Milgrim mausoleum. They were reckoning without Homer and there would be a cruel awakening. They had their lumps coming.

Homer was genial and extroverted but he was nobody's mark. Lieutenant Remington was right; a man doesn't get to be a millionaire by slapping people on the back.

I glanced once more toward my love and my aunt without success. I wondered where Homer was, but if I asked them they would think I was trying to make up and I was too proud for that.

I went out quietly and turned my footsteps toward Beverly Drive.

A man named McAllister, she had said, though she had forgotten the name of the firm . . . .

The name of the firm was McAllister, Noyes and Adams and the middle-aged lady in the waiting room wanted to know if I had an appointment.

"No. You may tell Mr. McAllister that I'm working with Lieutenant Remington, and I'm sure he'll understand."

She looked at me doubtfully for a moment before rising and disappearing down a corridor.

In a few moments, she came back to tell me Mr. McAllister would see me.

He was a portly, genial man with reddish gray hair and he rose to welcome me as I entered his office. He said,

"Left the Rams for good, finally, have you?"

I nodded and smiled.

"Great," he said. "You were great. Sit down, Mr. Callahan."

I sat down and he said, "I suppose you want to talk about Miss Milgrim's will?"

"If it's not a breach of ethics, Mr. McAllister."

"Nothing of the kind," he assured me. "Though I might have strained them a little by not notifying Miss Thorne by now. However, I'm old enough and dignified enough to strain an ethic if it might help to solve a murder." He paused. "If it is murder."

"It looks less like it every hour," I told him, "but it doesn't seem likely it was anything else. Miss Thorne is the sole heir?"

He nodded.

"Did that seem—strange to you? I'm asking for a purely personal opinion, of course."

"The wishes of spinsters," he said, "seemed strange to me only in the first few years of my practice. As for theatrical people—" He shrugged resignedly.

"Miss Thorne was not always the only heir, I presume?"

He paused. "Originally, Miss Thorne was to divide the estate with Enrico Rivali. That was changed six months ago."

"And Everett was never named?"

"Yes. He still is, and perhaps I shouldn't have told you Miss Thorne is the *only* heir. Everett is to be left one dollar."

I smiled. "That was your suggestion?"

"Mr. Noyes's," he said.

"Was Everett in town when you were told to notify him about Miss Milgrim's death?"

"Yes. He had been in town for two weeks. I'm almost sure it is the first time he has been in this town in seven years."

"Odd, isn't it, that he should come at this time?"

Leonard McAllister stared thoughtfully at me but didn't commit himself.

"Perhaps," I suggested, "he heard something. Mary Mae might have written him."

McAllister shrugged. "I'm not an investigator, Mr. Callahan, only a simple country lawyer." He smiled. "I envy you. I envy your position, walking the tightrope between the law and the lawless."

"You could have been a criminal lawyer," I said, "and walked the same rope."

He sighed. "That was my plan. But Mother wouldn't hear of it. And now that she's dead, it's too late. Tell me, Mr. Callahan, are you doing exactly what you want to do?"

"Pretty close to it, I guess. Though I got into it out of hunger. My father was killed by a hoodlum."

"I've followed your career," he said. "I think, if you developed some finesse, you could be first-rate." He stood up. "Well, I've given you all I know."

I shook his hand and thanked him and went out. I knew more now than I had when I'd entered his office, but it didn't make the case any less muddy. It made the finger longer that was pointing at Rivali. The finger had always pointed at Rivali, though, and the police hadn't locked him up. There had to be a reason for that.

The little information I picked up in McAllister's office was my quota for the afternoon. The next three hours were as fruitless and frustrating as any afternoon I had ever spent on a quest. At five o'clock I went home.

There, I reclined on my threadbare studio couch in sullen futility. There wasn't much reason for me to regret my inefficiency as an investigator; the professional police weren't having any better success. But I felt guilty about taking Uncle Homer's money and delivering nothing.

I ran them all over in my mind, again and again, and

constantly returned to Rivali. If there was an entry point
into this maze, he seemed to be the percentage choice.

I made a cheese omelet for dinner and drank three cups
of coffee. There was a possibility I would be up late tonight,
and I was tired already.

At a little before seven o'clock, the old flivver was heading
for the borderline district in Brentwood. The ancient Packard
was parked in front, the Florida Mercury right behind it.

I drove past, to the next corner, turned around and parked
a half block from the house, facing in the same direction
as the two cars in front of Rivali's. I turned off the engine
and waited.

Enrico had warned me against Everett Milgrim; what was
he doing now, making new alliances? About fifty feet ahead
of me, a black sedan was parked, and I remembered that
Gnup had told me they were going to put a man on Milgrim.

This wasn't a police car, however, and I wondered if
Gnup had sent a man in his own car. For there was a man
sitting behind the wheel and he, too, seemed to be waiting.
Brentwood would not be within the Beverly Hills Department jurisdiction.

In a few minutes, the light went on over Rivali's front
door and a man who resembled Everett Milgrim came down
the walk and went over to the Merc.

When the Merc pulled away, the car in front of me waited
until the Merc was a block away. Then it followed, not
showing any lights until the Merc had turned a corner.

I stayed where I was. And stayed and stayed and
stayed . . . .

At eight-thirty, a dark figure came down from the un-
lighted doorway and got behind the wheel of the Packard.
I gave him a full block's start.

It was an easy car to follow and I let him extend his lead
once we were in the traffic of San Vicente Boulevard. I

kept him in sight all the way to Hollywood.

And there, in front of a weathered, four-unit stucco building, the Packard parked. In the glow from the street light, I watched Enrico Rivali head for the entrance of the building that housed the hungry but immortal John Davenport.

This was a new development. What could these two have in common? The cinema. What else?

I could see shadows moving in the light showing through a window toward the rear of the apartment building, and it seemed to me that would be about where Davenport's apartment was located. It was a warm night, with a desert wind; perhaps the window was open.

An occasional car passed on the street but otherwise there was no one in sight. I slid over and got out on the curb side and walked quietly along the building next door until I reached the lighted window. It was open about half a foot.

Though its tone was low, Rivali's voice was recognizable, but not his words.

Davenport's voice was equally low, but it was a trained voice. He said, "You're being absurd. I don't need you, Rivali; I've been working rather steadily. I don't need you or any doubtful money."

Rivali, then, and the only word I could distinguish was "fool."

And Davenport said quietly, "You'd better go. Right now."

No answer from Rivali. I hurried back to my car and was behind the wheel when he came out of the apartment building and climbed into his Packard.

He didn't head for Wilshire, but for Sunset Boulevard. I kept him in range. Through Hollywood, through the Strip, into Beverly Hills.

When he turned off between the stone pillars, I was far enough behind to prevent overrunning him. His headlights flashed off the Lombardy poplars as I slowed and parked for a few seconds, the engine turning.

When his headlights were no longer visible, I turned mine off and drove slowly up the driveway. As my eyes adjusted, it was easier to make out the outlines of the driveway and the bulk of the castle ahead. I parked a hundred yards from the drawbridge and walked up.

There was a light showing over the entrance to Miss Thorne's cottage. I stayed in the shadows as Enrico came into that light; I didn't move again until the door opened and he went inside.

Then, keeping to the shadows, I went around toward the window that had been undraped last night. Somewhere, a window was open, because I could hear Rivali's voice again and this time I made out a few words.

"Inheritance" was one and "prissy little schemer" were three more. And then he said, "Damn your black soul!" and I thought it might be the right time to come around to the front door in case Miss Thorne needed help.

I started that way and heard footsteps coming across the cobblestones of the court. I paused in the shadow of a worn and yellow palm tree, waiting for the footsteps to become more personalized. They were certainly in a hurry.

In a moment, he came into the light over the door and I saw that it was Raymond Yoshida. He pressed the bell button, waited only a few seconds, and then opened the door and went in.

I paused, wondering whether to go back toward the end window or head for the front door. Was Yoshida an ally or an enemy of Joyce's? Had he come to help her—or Rivali?

I started toward the window—and from behind, someone prodded what might have been the barrel of a pistol into my spine and said, "Don't move!"

I'd heard the voice before, but couldn't place it. I said humbly, "I'm not moving. Is that a gun you're holding?"

"Shut up!" the hoarse voice said, and I recognized it. It

was Rivali's roommate, the belligerent George Parkas.

"Easy now, George," I soothed him. "If your head hadn't hit that mantel, I wouldn't have hurt you. *Think*, George; let reason prevail."

"Shut up," he said again, "and don't move. Just keep your big Irish yap shut!"

I was silent wondering what his purpose was in holding me out here.

And then, with the gun still pressed against my spine, his left forearm came up to press against my Adam's apple, and he began to pull me backward.

I growled in protest but he pressed the gun in more savagely and my breath became labored and my heart began to pound. I didn't have too much time; I was already dizzy. I had to make some move before the blackout.

I twisted my head sideways, releasing for a second the pressure on my Adam's apple. And I bellowed for help at the top of my burning lungs.

The noise must have startled him, for he loosened his grip on my neck. I lurched backward, into the gun, trying to find his chin with the back of my head.

He was wise to that one; his head was well back, out of danger. An old army trick came to me, and I reached my right hand down toward where his legs joined, knowing the reaction to that. His head would automatically come forward as he arched his crotch away.

As his head came forward, my head went back once more, smashing into his advancing face.

It was his turn to bellow as I twisted free and dived headlong for the protection of some juniper. I could hear him scrambling after me as the needles of the bushes scratched my hands and rasped against my clothes.

From the direction of the front door Rivali called, "George—! Are you out there, George?"

"He's here," I called. "He's—"

A major error in defensive strategy. For George was indeed there, but until I had opened my big Irish yap, George had not been sure of where *I* was.

He found me. And the gun, or whatever it was he held, found me at the same time, right above the ear.

The stars went away and consciousness departed.

∞∞∞∞∞∞∞∞∞ *ELEVEN* ∞∞∞∞∞∞∞∞∞

GNUP CAME INTO the big room where I was waiting and said, "What in hell are you, a hypochondriac? It's only a little bump."

I had been applying ice to the little bump about the size of a cantaloupe; I had maybe been moaning a little. I glared at him and didn't answer.

"Cripes," he said. "A big man like you!"

"Talk about something you understand," I told him. "What have you been doing?"

"I'm rounding the whole stinking kit and caboodle up," he said. "We'll get them all face to face and see who's the biggest liar."

"What constitutes the kit and caboodle?" I asked quietly.

"All the people Rivali saw tonight and that couple Milgrim went to see, the Thornes."

"Was that your man following Milgrim?" I asked.

He nodded. "And you followed Rivali. Milgrim started from there, too. Well, I'd have to be a hell of a lot dumber than I am if I couldn't see that Rivali is the core of this mess and it's a cinch he hasn't been leveling with us."

A uniformed man came in then, and Rivali was with him. He glared at me, at Sergeant Gnup, and then went over to sit sullenly in one of a row of chairs along the wall.

"Where's his buddy, that Parkas?" Gnup asked.

The officer said, "No luck yet, Sergeant. We're working on it." He went out.

Gnup looked at Rivali. "Where's George?"

Rivali shrugged.

"He's probably out with some girl," I said.

Rivali glared at me.

Gnup said, "Once more, Rivali — where's your buddy?"

"No speaka da Eengleesh," Rivali said.

"You can always put him away on a morals charge," I told Gnup. "If he sits awhile, maybe he'll feel more like a citizen."

Rivali sneered at me. "Peeping Tom," he said. "Slant-head."

The Thornes came in, Blanche and Herbie, and looked wonderingly at all of us. Then Blanche saw me and smiled. "Mr. Callahan, I'm glad to see you here."

"Sit down, folks," I said. "Better sit over here."

They came over to sit on the chairs flanking me, across the room from Rivali.

Blanche stared thoughtfully at him for a moment, nodded doubtfully, and looked at me. In a stage whisper, she asked, "They've caught him, have they? They've got the goods on him?"

"Almost," I said. "We're waiting for some others."

"Joyce, too?" she asked.

I nodded.

She looked at the ice pack. "What happened to you?"

"I slipped out there in the corridor. Everett came to see you tonight, did he?"

She nodded, started to talk — and Gnup warned me, "I'll do the questioning here, Callahan."

Lieutenant Remington came in. He was wearing a dinner jacket; he had obviously been called from a party. His voice was a little thick. "Where's the rest of 'em?"

"On the way in, Lieutenant," Gnup answered. "Though we can't seem to locate Parkas."

"Oh?" Remington went over to stand in front of Rivali. "Where's your boy friend, Enrico?"

Rivali shrugged.

Remington's voice hardened. "I can get a complaint on you, you know, any time. Be smart, Enrico."

Rivali blushed. And then said, "So help me, Lieutenant, I don't know where he is. When I came out of Miss Thorne's place, he wasn't anywhere in sight."

"And what was he doing outside of Miss Thorne's place?"

"Waiting for me. I told him to wait in the car."

Yoshida came in with Joyce Thorne. Joyce saw her folks and came over quickly to sit next to her mother. Her mother took her hand and said something quietly.

Yoshida looked at Rivali, at us, and then took a chair some distance from all of us.

Joyce patted the chair next to her. "Over here, Raymond."

He smiled and shook his head.

John Davenport came in, surveyed us all with cool dignity, and asked Remington, "Would you be kind enough, Sergeant, to explain the reason for this imposition?"

"In due time, Mr. Davenport. However, the title is Lieutenant. Please be seated."

John Davenport looked at each of us doubtfully and chose me. I was kind of touched. He sat in the chair to my left and asked, "What's it all about?"

"*In due time*, Mr. Davenport," Remington repeated ominously.

Davenport sighed and leaned back in his chair. He stared mournfully at nothing.

Blanche leaned forward to say, "Hello, John. It's been a long time."

His face lightened. "Blanche Arden—? It is, it is—How are you, dear?"

"Happy. And you, John?"

"I'm working," he said. "Not much, but it's getting better. I got rid of Adler."

"Good," she said.

Gnup whirled around. "Who's Adler? What do you mean, you got rid of him?"

"My former agent," Davenport explained wearily. "I fired him, Lieutenant. Sidney Adler, the world's worst agent."

"I'm not a lieutenant," Gnup said.

"Persevere," Davenport advised him. "Study and work. It will come."

I smiled. Gnup looked at me and I stopped smiling. I asked, "Is this the kit and caboodle, now?"

"Not quite," Gnup said.

Then the door opened once more and Milgrim came in.

"Now," Gnup said. And to the Lieutenant, "All here, sir."

"Except for Parkas," the Lieutenant reminded him.

Gnup sighed and said nothing.

"All right," Remington conceded. "We'll start." He told Milgrim, "Sit anywhere."

Milgrim went over to sit next to Rivali as Remington and Gnup came over to stand in front of Davenport.

Gnup asked, "Did Enrico Rivali come to see you to-night?"

Davenport nodded. "He phoned around six and came after eight. He told me, over the phone, that he was planning a picture. Well, in my palmier days, I didn't deal with anyone as morally degraded and aesthetically barren as Enrico Rivali." Davenport looked sad. "However, this is today, so I permitted him to come to my apartment."

Across the room, Rivali growled. Davenport glanced at him and back to Gnup.

Remington asked, "And is that what you talked about, a prospective picture?"

"Vaguely," Davenport said. He glanced uncomfortably at me. "Mr. Rivali had a—a plan. He happened to know that a Mr. Homer Gallup was an ardent fan of mine, and he hoped, thereby, to use me to wheedle the required capital from Mr. Gallup. I—should have expected something of the sort. I told him to leave."

"And that's all?"

Davenport nodded. "That is every sordid detail."

Both Gnup and Remington moved along the line and now stood in front of Blanche and Herbie Thorne. Gnup said, "Everett Milgrim came to see you. Why?"

Blanche Arden Thorne licked her lips nervously. "We're not rightly sure, Sergeant. He kept talking about being cheated out of his inheritance, as though we had something to do about that. He said he'd make a settlement now with us, or create some kind of scandal later. I just couldn't make head or tail out of what he was saying, Sergeant." She looked up hopefully. "Did Mary Mae leave us some money, or something?"

Gnup didn't answer. Both he and Remington turned around and stared at Everett Milgrim. Remington said, "Well, Milgrim—?"

"I have no idea why Mrs. Thorne is lying," Everett said. "I simply went out there to see if they knew anything about the will. My sister's attorneys have been extremely unco-operative. I have urgent business in Florida and need to leave town unless there is some important reason for my staying here."

"Don't you call me a liar, you snake!" Blanche Thorne said. She half rose.

Joyce put a hand on her arm and said something quietly to her.

Remington said, "And now you, Miss Thorne. What did Rivali want with you?"

"Blackmail," Joyce Thorne said evenly. Her chin went up.

Rivali rose, muttering in Italian. Remington turned and gestured him down. He turned back and said, "Go on."

Joyce Thorne took a deep breath. "He said he knew I would inherit some of Miss Milgrim's money. He said there was a scandal in my background that would be revealed unless I financed a picture for him with some of that money." She stopped and stared at the floor.

Lieutenant Remington asked gently, "Are you Miss Milgrim's heir?"

Joyce looked up. "Not that I know of. Oh, perhaps she left me a few dollars, but certainly she wouldn't leave me enough to finance a motion picture."

"And the scandal?" Remington persisted. "Would you rather reveal it privately?"

"There isn't any to reveal," Joyce said firmly. "I hadn't the faintest idea what he was talking about."

From the other side of the room, Rivali said, "Humph!"

Little Herbie Thorne stood up and started over toward him. Gnup moved quickly to intercept him. Herbie sat down again.

"And then he threatened me, calling me names," Joyce went on levelly. "Well, I've been wary of prowlers, lately, so Mr. Yoshida wired a buzzer system from the cottage to his apartment over the garage. I summoned him that way and he came over. Then we heard this shout outside and we all went out—and there was Mr. Callahan, unconscious."

"As usual," Gnup added, and chuckled.

Remington glanced bleakly at him and questioningly at me.

I said, "I couldn't call any of them liars so far, Lieutenant."

"I can," he said gruffly. He moved back a step and his gaze went from person to person. "All I've had is lies so far. I'm going to warn you people that we know a lot more about you than you've been willing to reveal. This isn't working. If we have to stay here all night, we will. We're going to start over and question each one of you individually and privately."

Blanche said softly. "Couldn't Herbie and I be questioned together, Lieutenant? Herbie gets nervous, away from me."

"Perhaps," Remington said acidly, "he'll get nervous enough to tell us the truth. All right, we'll start with—" he looked around the room—"we'll start with you, Rivali. Go with Sergeant Gnup."

Then Remington looked at me. "You can't check any of them, Brock?"

I said, "From what I overheard Mr. Davenport telling Rivali, his explanation seemed logical."

"Okay," Remington said. "He'll need a ride home, anyway. You can take him now. Unless you want to stay for this circus—?"

"No, thanks. My head is killing me. I'll bet it's a concussion. I'll take Davenport home and check back in the morning." I stood up. "You can hold Rivali for a while, can't you? He's the key, I'm sure."

"We can try," he said. "He's sent for an attorney. He's sharing one with Milgrim. I'd like to be there when those two try to outfumble each other for the lawyer's bill."

We went out, the immortal John and I. "What a despicable and avaricious creature that Rivali is," he murmured. "I'm amazed that he hasn't prospered out here."

"Maybe his timing is bad," I suggested. My head throbbed in time with my footsteps; my vision was blurry.

"You're stumbling," Davenport said. "Is something wrong?"

"I've a blinding headache. I got bopped tonight. By George Parkas. The fresh air will help."

We went out and over to my flivver.

We were under way when he said, "By Parkas? What happened?"

"Oh, a private feud."

A silence of two blocks, and then: "Why were you listening to my talk with Rivali? Is there a microphone in my apartment?"

"No microphone. I was following Enrico, not you. I listened outside your open window."

"But aren't you working on Mary Mae's murder? What connection could *my* visit with Rivali have with Mary Mae's murder?"

"I have no idea. It seems clear that Rivali is mixed up in it somewhere, so I padded along behind him, checking *everybody* he had reason to visit with."

A longer silence, now, a four-block silence. And then John Davenport asked, "And why did you lie to clear me with Lieutenant Remington?"

I didn't answer.

"If you were listening," Davenport explained, "you know we never mentioned Homer Gallup's name. I told the Lieutenant we had."

I said nothing, hoping he'd go on.

"Are you trying to protect her too?" he asked.

"Why not?" I said.

He sighed. "Yes. Of course. Why not? A girl with a CPA's mind and an agent's heart, but beautiful, isn't she? Why not?"

"If you think that about her," I asked, "why are you trying to protect her?"

"Because I love them," he said. "Young and old, ugly and beautiful, short or tall, fat or slim, I love them all so long as they're female."

"We're brothers," I said. "Blood brothers. How could Rivali hope to get money out of her?"

"He thinks she's going to inherit. Some time ago, he and Joyce were co-heirs, evidently, but then Rivali and Mary Mae had this falling out, he claims, and he's sure he was cut out of her will."

"When did he become sure of that?"

"Who knows? Who can ever know, with that man?"

"If it's true," I said, "one will get you twenty he didn't know it before Mary Mae died."

John Davenport expelled his breath and said nothing.

"And now," I said, "that you've admitted the meeting wasn't for the purpose of hooking Homer Gallup, why did Rivali come to you?"

"He wants me for the picture," Davenport said wearily. "Despite what I think of him, Rivali has always been in my fan club. And so has Miss Thorne."

"And the scandal he threatened her with? Were you to use it on her?"

"I was. And he told me what it was, and you can ask from now until doomsday, and I won't tell you."

"It could be connected with murder," I pointed out. "You're a citizen first, Mr. Davenport."

"My friends call me Jack," he said.

"Okay, Jack—level."

"Never," he said. "If you were listening, didn't you hear it?"

"I heard almost nothing," I said. "But thanks for the information." I turned onto Kenmore. "How can you sleep tonight knowing you might be shielding a murderer?"

His laugh was ironic. "Oh God—forty years in Hollywood and the man wants to know, how can I sleep tonight? Callahan, even amateurs like Judas slept."

I stopped in front of his apartment building. "All right. Good night and good luck."

He climbed out and held the door open for a moment. "Good luck to you. Try to think well of me, won't you? I've always been an admirer of yours."

"Good night," I said again. "Good night, *citizen!*"

He closed the door and I gunned off, though that's nothing spectacular in my old flivver. The tires didn't squeal; only the engine complained.

I turned into the bright lights and swirling carbon monoxide of Sunset Boulevard, the street of stars, the treadmill of tourists, the winding, grinding, noisy street that leads where all streets lead—to the grave.

Through Hollywood, through the Strip, through Beverly Hills to Westwood, where I live. And there I slept without dreams.

ssssssssssss *TWELVE* ssssssssssss

IN THE MORNING, I looked at the pictures I had picked up from the lunch counter but they triggered nothing. I fried five eggs and made half a dozen slices of toast. That, with a quart of milk, was my breakfast.

The *Times* had the story of last night's roundup, but no mention of my having been hit on the head. I hadn't seen any reporters around when I left; perhaps this story was a Remington press release. He was quoted as saying: "An interesting pattern of deceit and intrigue has been uncovered." He didn't say what it was and I had a hunch he had enjoyed very little interrogatory luck with Rivali.

And I doubted if I would. Even if I had conned Rivali into thinking I would co-operate with him, he would have been too wary to confide in me. I was glad I had put him on the opposite side of the fence.

Miss Thorne, now—I had not put her on the opposite side of the fence. Perhaps, this morning, she would confide in me. I took two aspirin and drove over there.

Wallace Darrow's sumptuous Cadillac was parked near the entrance to the cottage. I pulled in behind him and made a lot of noise slamming the door of my car before going up to ring her bell. Though there wasn't any dew on Wallace's car.

Joyce Thorne looked tired this morning. "What now?"

she asked. "More questions? I haven't any answers."

I smiled at her. "I was going by and felt the urgent need for a cup of coffee. You make fine coffee."

"Come in," she said. "Mr. Darrow is here. He's just proposed to me."

Darrow was sitting in the living room. He must have overheard us, because he stared at her accusingly.

"Good morning, Mr. Darrow," I said. "Up early aren't you?"

"Not particularly." He rose. "Okay, Joyce. Sorry I intruded." He stood there like a dog waiting for a bone.

"You're forgiven," she said coolly. "Good luck with your career."

He looked at her, at me, back at her, and then gave us a view of his back as he stalked out.

Joyce looked at me and shrugged.

"You can be nasty, can't you?" I asked.

"I imagine he can too," she said. "The coffee is in the kitchen."

There, we sat at the kitchen table and I asked, "If you're nervous here all alone, why don't you have your folks come and stay with you for a while?"

"They wouldn't leave their flowers," she said, *their precious damned flowers!*" Her hand shook as she poured me a cup of coffee.

"He's the man," I said, "you identified as a producer night before last. I mean Darrow is. Why did you lie?"

"I didn't. I had a half-date with Wallace and a half-date with this producer and the producer phoned while you were here. Now you can believe that or not; it's a matter of total indifference to me." She poured her own coffee. "Have you made your explanation to Miss Bonnet yet?"

I said nothing. I could feel myself blush.

"You," she said. "You and your fine talk. The king-sized Lochinvar. You don't fool me."

"I don't fool anybody," I admitted humbly. "I'm a bumbling amateur in a highly professional business."

She looked up from her coffee. "Migawd, you're blushing!"

I said nothing.

She took a deep breath. "What's going on? What is all the intrigue about? Why would Wallace Darrow propose to me? Tell me, Brock Callahan, am I going to inherit more than I thought?"

"I have no idea," I said. That was no lie; I didn't actually *know* how much she thought she was going to inherit.

"And you accuse *me* of lying," she said bitterly.

I said nothing.

"And last night you were spying on me," she went on. "Why?"

"I didn't spy on you. I was following Rivali. Did he admit anything to the police last night?"

"I don't know," she said. "We were all questioned separately."

"Do you want to tell me what this scandal is that he threatened you with?"

She shook her head. "Even if I knew, I wouldn't want to tell you. What are you to me, Brock Callahan?"

"I think I could be a friend," I answered.

"Could you? And are you loyal to your friends?"

I nodded.

"Isn't Miss Bonnet a friend?" she asked.

"Quit playing the village virgin," I said. "It takes two to tango."

She glared at me and her eyes misted over.

"If you're in danger," I said, "I want to be a friend. If you're in trouble, it's possible I can help. But we both know, don't we, that you haven't confided completely in me?"

"I don't know what you know and I don't really care,"

she said wearily. "Your leaden charm no longer overwhelms me. Why don't you finish your coffee and go?"

I stood up without finishing my coffee. I said, "Somewhere, you will have to find a friend. You're obviously in the middle of a mess, Joyce."

"I have friends," she said. "Friends I haven't even used yet. You can find your way out, I'm sure."

I went out and closed the door quietly behind me. I was halfway down the walk to the court when I met Homer.

"Well," I said. "Forget your key again?"

He shook his head and looked at me grimly. "I saw your car. What's going on here, Brock?"

"I was trying to question Miss Thorne. She was uncooperative. It will all be in your report."

"All—?" he asked. "Brock, Jan's upset. That sweet little girl is *sick* about the way you're acting."

"That sweet little girl won't even talk to me," I said. "Nor will your unsweet little wife. Whose side are you on, Homer?"

"I don't get you."

"It's the men versus the women, isn't it? No matter what other battles are current, it's *always* the boys against the girls, isn't it? I sure as hell shouldn't have to tell a Texan that."

"Cripes," he said. He looked worriedly at the ground.

"You amaze me," I said. "A big boy like you—"

He sighed. "I guess I lost my balance for a second there. But that Jan, Brock—I mean, how many are there like *her?*"

"Only one her age," I answered. "Aunt Sheila's older. Jeepers, Homer, how many do you want like those two?"

He smiled and then he chuckled. And then he laughed. He clapped me on the back and said, "Carry on, buddy. I hope to hell you know what you're doing."

"I don't. I'm not bright, Homer, only persistent. Did Yoshida tell Jan I was parked there all night?"

"No. Yoshida came through like a man. He said you had arrived only half an hour before us. But Jan doesn't believe him."

"Isn't that just like a woman? They ask, but don't believe. Are they here now?"

Homer shook his head. "They're shopping for furniture. I only came over to look at my house before they begin to ruin it."

I left him there and went down to Headquarters. In the intensive grilling those people had gone through last night, surely Gnup and Remington must have learned *something* new.

If they had, it would have to wait. Because Gnup was hurrying out as I came up toward the front of the building, and he said, "I've just got the word on that coniine. Solid, too; good enough to take into court."

"On who bought it, you mean?"

He nodded impatiently. "Rivali. I'm going over to pick him up. Want to come along?"

"I'll follow," I said, "In my car."

Another detective was already waiting in a Department car, the engine running. They were out of sight by the time I was underway, but I knew the route.

If I had gone in his car and they were delayed, I would have been stuck with them. This is an area with very little public transportation.

Rivali. . . . All along, the finger had pointed at him. In most murder cases, the obvious is true, but the standard cases do not usually come to the direct attention of the private investigators. Men in my despised profession usually deal only with the devious and the deviates, and there are rarely any obvious conclusions to be drawn from the shenanigans of these kinds of people.

Not that Rivali was standard. But he was the most obviously *evil* of the people I had interrogated and the most obviously capable of any crime that would further his career or protect his interests.

The two aspirin hadn't killed my headache. I rubbed the bump above my ear and it seemed to be smaller this morning, but the headache it had fostered had diminished only a little.

I hoped Parkas would be at the house and would give me some excuse for slugging him.

The old flivver pulled into Rivali's block just as the Department car stopped in front of his house. I parked behind it and Gnup waited for me, the other detective staying in the car. We went up through the cacti together to the front door.

The Packard was in the garage but there was no sound in the house. Until Sergeant Gnup rang the door chimes. And silence followed that.

"His car is there," I said.

Gnup nodded and rang the chime again.

From inside we could hear the shuffle of hesitant footsteps, and then the door opened and the puffed, red-eyed face of George Parkas looked out at us mournfully.

"We want to see Rivali," Gnup said.

Parkas' voice was slightly above a whisper. "He's not here. He's gone."

"Gone where?"

Parkas shrugged.

"His car is here," Gnup said. "We're coming in, Parkas. We'll see if he's gone."

"You're not coming in," Parkas said. "He's gone. You're not coming." He looked at me. "He can't come in without a warrant, can he?"

I didn't answer that. I asked, "Are you sick? What's the matter with you? Your face is all puffed up."

He looked back at Gnup without answering me. He said, "You're not coming in, not without a warrant. Try it, and see."

Gnup said, "All right. I'll get a warrant. And you'll come with me, now, while I get one. Come on."

Parkas shook his head dully. "No."

"Move!" Gnup said, and his hand went in under his jacket.

The door slammed in our faces as Gnup pulled the gun. It was a heavy door. I tried the knob. It was a locked, heavy door.

Gnup stared at me doubtfully.

"You're out of your jurisdiction," I said. "This is Los Angeles. If you want to go in here, you'd better drop in at the West Side Station first."

He nodded. "There's something fishy here. He looked— punchy."

"He always has, to me. Maybe he's got a cold."

Gnup put his gun back in its holster. "Would you stay here? Would you watch the house while I go over to the West Side Station?"

I nodded.

"Are you armed?" he asked.

I shook my head. "I don't need to be. I'll be careful."

"All right. Stay right here, in the yard."

He hurried back to his car and I stood where I was for about a minute. When he was gone, when the car had turned out of sight, I left the front porch and went around the side of the house.

There was a window open a few inches here, and through it I could hear the low, mournful voice of George Parkas. "Gone," he was saying. "Gone where? Gone. You bastards—Oh, you dirty bastards! He's gone away. He's left me. Gone, gone, gone—"

The window was too high for me to see into; I went quietly along to the back of the house. A small service porch jutted out from the kitchen door, but the door to it was locked. I pulled a redwood bench over to a spot below the high kitchen window and climbed up on that.

I could see through the kitchen, but all I could see of George Parkas was one shoulder. If my memory of the house was accurate, he was sitting in the dining room.

Sitting—? On what? His shoulder was too low for him to be sitting on a chair. Was he sitting on the floor? And now I could see one foot and it was clear to me he wasn't sitting. He was kneeling, kneeling on the floor.

I went back to the partly open window at the side of the house, taking the redwood bench along. I had set it down and was about to climb up onto it, when a voice behind me said, "What's going on, young man?"

I turned to face a thin and vinegar-faced woman of about sixty who was standing on the other side of the hedge that divided this property from the house next door.

"I'm not sure, ma'am," I said, "but I hope to find out."

"Well, I'm calling the police, in case you're interested," she said.

"A good idea, ma'am," I assured her. "The Beverly Hills Police have authorized me to investigate here. But you'd better phone, anyway."

I stood up on the bench and the odor of incense came through the few inches of open window. I stood on tiptoe, but all I could see was the upper two thirds of the far wall of this room. I would need to get higher still. From inside, George's voice sounded shaky and sick. He was talking some foreign tongue, undoubtedly Greek, and it sounded like praying to me.

I clambered down again and decided not to pry any more. It seemed clear to me that George wasn't going anywhere.

In a few more minutes, Gnup came with an officer from the West Side Station. I told them what I had heard and smelled.

"Jesus--!" Gnup said. He looked at the Packard and at me. "What do you think?"

"What's there left to think, Sergeant?"

Gnup looked at the L.A. officer. "It's a heavy door."

"So? The latch would still be the same size, probably. A foot should do it. Especially in a house as old as this."

"In the interest of jurisdiction," Gnup said, "will it be your foot?"

"Let's go," the man said.

We all went up on the porch. He stood back from the door as Gnup and his partner took their guns out. He lifted his foot and crashed it forward at a spot a few inches to the left of the knob.

It was an old house. The door swung open.

Gnup went in first; I, last.

George Parkas was still on his knees in the dining room and the air was sickening-sweet with incense. There were flowers at both ends of the heavy dining-room table, flowers in great vases above the head and below the feet of the body of Enrico Rivali.

Parkas had stopped praying. He was now crying.

THIRTEEN

I HADN'T HAD lunch and my stomach was growling. In the smoke-filled room, my head pulsated in a nagging, stomach-unsettling throb. Reporters were there and Remington; Gnup, along with some men from this station, was still interrogating George Parkas in another room.

A photographer from the *Times* put his lens a few feet from my nose and his flash-bulb flare was torture. I tried not to look annoyed. In this town, the *Times* can do no wrong.

Remington was saying to Captain Devine, "It all ties in with the Milgrim murder, Captain. We'd like to have Parkas as soon as you're finished with him here."

"All right, all right!" Devine said irritably. "Will you boys with the cameras please get the hell out now?"

A reporter from the *Mirror-News* asked me, "What did you think of, Callahan, when you saw Rivali on the table like that?"

"I thought he was dead," I said.

"Naturally. I mean, kind of weird, wasn't it? This Parkas is a homo, right? Rivali, too?"

"Not to my knowledge," I said. "I guess they're just close, like the *Times* and the *Chicago Tribune*."

A uniformed man came in and handed Captain Devine a sheet of paper. I stood up and my headache almost floored me. I stood for a second in blind agony and then walked slowly over to where the Captain was handing the paper to Lieutenant Remington.

Remington finished reading it and said to me, "Coniine. Damn it, where does that put us? He sure as hell wasn't a suicide, was he? Same damned killer, the way it looks."

"Maybe not," I said. "Captain, may I leave now? I'm sick, and food might help it. I've got to eat."

Devine took a deep breath. "Okay, okay. But listen, Callahan, this isn't Beverly Hills. We don't want private peepers messing around murder cases in this town. So keep your nose clean."

I stood there glaring at him.

"Watch it," he said. "Now watch your tongue."

"You're new," I said softly, "new to the West Side and to your captaincy. Why don't you phone downtown and ask about me?"

His eyes were blank. "Is that so? Who should I call, downtown?"

"Anyone," I answered. "You could start with the Chief of Police, if you wanted to. I'll wait. I can wait that long."

Remington said soothingly, "Captain, Mr. Callahan is a little special. He's worked hard for his reputation."

One of the reporters said, "Hell, yes, Captain. He's a big-shot ex-Ram. Take it easy with him."

The Captain flushed. I looked at the reporter and he sneered. My head throbbed and a surge of irrationality moved through me and I took a step toward the reporter.

Remington stepped swiftly between us. His back was to me as he told the reporter, "Why don't you leave? Why don't you leave while you're alive and whole?"

The rest of the newspapermen in the room were muttering now. Small men working for big papers and it gave them a false sense of their own importance. Meaningless men with powerful weapons.

My headache dimmed and sharpened, dimmed and sharpened. Through it, I heard Captain Devine say, "All right now Lieutenant. Let's not fly off the handle."

"I'll go quietly," I said. "You calm them. I don't need the slobs. I never needed them."

I went out to a farewell of catcalls and boos. They knew I didn't need them and therefore wasn't afraid of them. They hated anybody who wasn't afraid of them. Because they were such small men in jobs too big for them.

I stopped at the nearest drugstore and took four aspirin with three glasses of water. Then I drove over to my own favorite drugstore for lunch.

By the time I got there, my headache had diminished and my fan was back to work, ready with a smile and a good word. This man I needed.

"You look sick," he said. "How about some poached eggs?"

"I had eggs for breakfast," I told him. "Some soup first."

The soup was thick and creamy potato soup and the rumbling in my stomach went away. I ate my steak slowly, thinking of Enrico Rivali.

In my mind, I saw him again on that massive table with the flowers, laid out in ceremonial display. I wondered if a priest had reached him in time. There probably had been some things Rivali had to confess, though he must have left the church long ago.

I dawdled over my coffee, killing time.

By the time I got to Beverly Hills Headquarters, Gnup was back. He sat in a small room with his notes, looking like a mouse in a maze.

"It was all sewed up," he said. "All sewed up in my mind, at least. Rivali—who else? And if he'd been shot, still Rivali. But a man isn't likely to take his own poison, is he?"

"Maybe. If he's cornered. What did Parkas tell you?"

"He found him like that, this morning, in his car in the garage. All right, Rivali left here about two o'clock last night. Seven o'clock this morning Parkas finds him out in the car, poisoned by his own coniine. Where do we start?"

"All over again at the beginning," I answered. "Where was Parkas last night, when we were looking for him?"

"In Venice, with one of his—boy friends. He and Rivali had had a quarrel and Parkas had gone to another—friend, in spite, the way I read it. Though he didn't admit it that—bluntly. Well, early this morning, Parkas gets an attack of conscience, hurries home to his own true love—and finds him in the car, dead."

"Maybe," I said. "Or maybe, still hating him, killed him?"

Gnup shook his head. "It doesn't look like it. There's still some checking to do in the lab, but from where we sit, no."

"How about the Packard? Prints?"

"They're still working on it. What was that fuss you had with the vultures of the press?"

"Nothing. I was sick and unreasonable and they were well and unreasonable."

Gnup shook his head. "I don't understand you. What's the percentage in getting the newspapers down on you?"

Newspapers. . . . Again that flash of near-knowledge and I thought of those pictures and the lead that had almost come to the surface.

"What are you thinking now?" Gnup asked. "You looked almost intelligent there for a second."

"I'm thinking about newspapers, for some reason," I said. "I wish I knew the reason."

He said nothing.

"Coniine," I said. "How many people have access to coniine?"

"If you got enough money," Gnup said, "you can get

anything, even more money."

"Not amateurs," I argued. "They wouldn't know where to start. Figure this, where did we concentrate? Who was the hub? Who was the focal point of all our investigation?"

"Rivali."

"Right. But who was the real hub?"

"You tell me."

"Mary Mae Milgrim. Everything begins and ends with her; it always comes back to her."

"You tell me how to question a corpse," Gnup said, "and I'll get right on it."

"Newspapers," I said. "Newspapers, newspapers, newspapers—"

"How much?" Gnup said wearily. "I'll buy one, if it will shut you up."

"Newspapers," I said, "and Mary Mae Milgrim. I think I've almost got it."

"Confide," he said. "We're working together."

"It's not there yet," I said, "not completely." I stood up. "You're still holding Parkas, of course?"

"He isn't ours to hold," Gnup said. "Captain Devine out at the West Lost Angeles Station made that very, very clear. He's probably free by now."

"He can't be," I said. "He's a dangerous man in his present state of mind. He has to be held."

"You argue with Captain Devine then. I tried. To hell with the L.A.P.D."

"You're making noises like a Santa Monica officer," I said. "You're not positive that Captain Devine released him, are you?"

"No." He pointed at a phone. "Why don't you ask?"

I phoned the W.L.A. Station and got Devine. I said, "This is Brock Callahan, Captain. I wondered if you were still holding George Parkas."

"For a few minutes yet. Why?"

"Because it would be dangerous to release him. He probably knows who killed his friend and George is not exactly
a normal man."

"If he knew, he'd tell us, wouldn't he? You're not making
sense, Callahan. Unless you got some information we should
have."

"None, Captain. But I urge you to—"

"Listen, peeper," he said, "don't try to tell me my business. If Parkas knew anything, we'd have it. This isn't
Beverly Hills."

"Aren't you even going to put a man on him?"

"You stick to your knitting, Callahan." The line went
dead.

I replaced the phone and stared at Gnup's smile. "He
likes you too," I said.

"He's too young for the job," Gnup said. "He'll learn,
maybe. If he doesn't tangle with the wrong man."

"He already has," I said.

Gnup chuckled. "Phone your friends downtown and see.
Come on, I dare you."

"I don't use my influence petulantly," I said with dignity.
"Well, I've got to get to work."

"Work?" he said. "Where?"

"I'm going down to see my friends," I said.

He frowned. "Headquarters? Downtown?"

"Downtown," I admitted. "My good friends at the
Times."

He laughed. "Oh, boy! Oh, dear God—"

Well, it's a big paper and its right hand can't be sure
about its left, though there is probably nothing to the left
on the *Los Angeles Times,* not even a hand. The only place
where we agreed.

Their morgue is complete and well indexed; despite the
men who write for it, it is one hell of an efficient newspaper,

and their coverage, except for important news, is as good as any in America.

And there, in those vast files, I ran across a name I hadn't heard for a decade, a name that had been as big as Louella Parsons and Hedda Hopper were today. Even bigger than Hedda and equal with Parsons—a girl named Dawn Rhodes, though it probably was a pseudonym.

She knew where the bodies were buried, that girl, and she had the wit and the flare to make her columns something better than the puff sheets they were today. She was a *writer,* God bless her.

I went out of the big building on First Street and into the smog, wondering if Dawn Rhodes was still around and available.

It took some doing, finding her. I had a newspaperman friend, believe it or not, and he referred me to another one who referred me to another one.

And by the time I started out for Santa Monica, the traffic was solid and the smog only a hairsbreadth from a number one alert. The headache was back. Man, it was back. . . .

Nausea moved tenuously in me and I was tempted to breathe deeply to quell it, but that smog would only put me over the edge. I fought to keep my vision clear and my stomach stable and drove on doggedly.

Past the Veterans Administration grounds, the sea air began to blow into the car and the nausea vanished. Even my headache diminished some as the flivver plowed along, getting closer to the sea.

She lived in an old mansion on Ocean Front that had been turned into apartments. She lived in a front apartment, with a view of the Santa Monica Bay.

She opened her door and looked up at me quizzically, a white-haired woman, thin as a hummingbird, with bright blue eyes and a jaunty little chin.

"Brock Callahan, ma'am," I said. "Came to pay you a visit."

"It isn't," she said, and then her face lightened. "By God, it is, the great Callahan."

"You know me, ma'am?"

"Know you—? Three consecutive years All-League with the Rams and an All-American at Stanford. Is there someone in this silly city who doesn't know *you?*" She held the door wide. "Come in, come in."

I came into a living room furnished in bright provincial with a big bay window opening onto the ocean.

"One doesn't forget a champion, Miss Rhodes," I said. I sat on a flowered, softly cushioned davenport. "And you were a champion."

"Blarney," she said. "You've got that, too, haven't you?" She sat in a pull-up chair and looked at me anxiously. "You seem a little peaked. Are you?"

I rubbed my forehead. "Yes. A headache. I got bumped on the head last night in that fracas over at Miss Milgrim's old place."

She stared at me. "Are you working on that case, on the death of Mary Mae?"

I nodded.

"Terrible thing," she said. "Terrible. And on the radio, a little while ago, I heard about Enrico Rivali. I guess nobody will mourn him."

"George Parkas will," I said.

She frowned. "Who's he?"

"An ex-wrestler. A bit player. A—friend of Enrico's."

"Oh," she said, and grimaced in disgust. "Oh, I see."

I rubbed my forehead.

She said quietly, "And now you've come here to talk about Mary Mae."

"If you want to, Miss Rhodes. Only if you want to."

"I don't know if I want to or not," she said thoughtfully. "I'll have to think a minute about that. And while I'm thinking, I can make you a cup of strong tea. Best thing in the world for a headache." She rose and went out.

I relaxed on the soft davenport in the pleasant room, thinking back to the good days when the industry was alive in Hollywood and the stars were stars, not people. Before the government had moved into everybody's pockets, there was money made out here, made and spent on the grand scale.

When Dawn Rhodes came back with my tea, I thanked her and asked, "The stars were different in the old days, weren't they?"

"They had less talent," she admitted, "but I don't think they were very different. The entertainment profession has always been a degraded and dissolute field, you know. They were never much, but I think they were more fun in the old days."

"Mary Mae, now," I said. "She was about as untalented as any of them, wasn't she?"

Dawn Rhodes sighed and nodded. "I've seen snips on half-hour TV Westerns with three times Mary Mae's talent." She pointed at the cup in my hand. "Drink."

I drank. "Good," I said. "I don't know why I don't drink more tea."

"It's wonderful stuff," she said. "What do you want to know about Mary Mae?"

"Something that might help me find out who killed her."

"Rivali killed her, didn't he? Wasn't he in her will?"

"All right. Then who killed Rivali?"

"Didn't he kill himself? Knowing the police were closing in on him, wouldn't Rivali kill himself? It's logical, if you knew the man."

"It's logical, but I don't think he did. You knew something about Mary Mae, didn't you? I read in one of your columns of many Julys ago a hint that you knew something about Mary Mae Milgrim.''

''You're a clever man, Mr. Callahan,'' she said. ''I had no idea guards could be so discerning.''

''Then you do know something?''

She shook her head. ''I didn't *know* anything then. I only suspected it. And I've always been sorry I wrote that bit. Because Mary Mae, before Rivali soured her, was a pretty damned sweet kid.''

''Imitation Southern belle and all,'' Dawn Rhodes went on, after a pause, ''Mary Mae had good instincts and firm loyalties. How often do you find that out here?''

''I don't know. Rarely, I imagine.''

''Almost never. Why should I demean her memory now?''

''To help find a killer.''

''The killer's dead,'' she said. ''We agree on that, don't we?''

''No. In order to be sure, we have to know why. And when we know why, perhaps we'll learn that the killer isn't dead. Mary Mae never married, did she?''

''Never. She was loyal, as I've said. She only had room for one love in one life.''

I said nothing, waiting. I sipped my tea and the headache lessened.

She said, ''What are you waiting for, the word?''

I nodded.

Her bright blue eyes moved past me, staring at the wall, staring at yesterday. ''Maybe I don't know anything. A girl tries so hard to find something controversial to write about, she can sometimes find something where there's actually nothing.''

''Not Dawn Rhodes,'' I said.

''Dawn Rhodes,'' she told me, ''is an old lady sitting in

the sun in Santa Monica, watching the sea gulls. I've stopped making trouble."

"I hope not," I said. "When a human stops making trouble, it means he has stopped being involved. And when you're not involved in life, you're dead."

"No," she said. "False and shallow, that kind of thinking. And you know it. That's the motto of the phony liberals, that trouble kick. Who is Albert Schweitzer making trouble for? Is he dead?"

I sipped my tea. Great stuff, warming and strengthening.

"No," she said. "Let's talk about the Rams."

"No," I said. "All right. You didn't know anything. And you didn't suspect anything. But if you were Mary Mae, or a star in the same spot, where would you have gone, that July long ago?"

A long silence, a long, long silence. The tea was finished and my headache almost gone. In this quiet room, we could hear the waves washing on the shore and we could see the whitecaps from Palos Verdes to Point Dume.

Finally she said, "It's near Camarillo. It's called the Village Sanitarium." She sighed. "They still go there, I hear."

∽∽∽∽∽∽∽∽ *FOURTEEN* ∽∽∽∽∽∽∽∽

At the beverly Hills Hotel, I found a parking space some distance from the portico. I could have driven right to the portico and an attendant would have parked the car, but they do it in such a sneering way, because of the age of my flivver.

I went up to the suite occupied by the Gallups without announcing myself from the desk.

My Aunt Sheila opened the door and said, "Well—!"

"Get off the morality binge, you unblushing bride," I told her gruffly. "Homer here?"

She moved back a half step and stared at me doubtfully.

"You make me sick," I said. "Is Homer here?"

"Brock!" she said. "What's got into you? Is that any way to talk to your aunt?"

"I'll respect your age when you act it," I told her. I walked in, and met Homer as he approached the door.

"You drunk?" he asked me.

"No. Rivali's dead."

He nodded. "I heard. Good riddance."

"I've got a lead," I said. "I want to talk to you about it."

"Sure, sure," he said. "Come in. I thought the police had tabbed Rivali for Mary Mae's death."

"So. And who killed Rivali then?"

He shrugged. "Does anyone care? Outside of the police?"

"I care."

He stared at me. "Sit down, Brock. Sheila, call room service and tell them to send up some of that Einlicher I stored down there."

"Like hell," my Aunt Sheila said. "Not for him. Did you hear the way he talked to me?"

"I heard," Homer said, "and it was about time. You and Miss Bonnet have appointed yourself a two-member morality commission and I don't think either one of you is qualified."

Sheila stared at him and he stared right back at Sheila. In about twenty seconds, she stopped staring and lifted the phone.

Homer turned to face me. "Now calm down. You came in here like that no-account Lieutenant Remington, throwing your weight around."

"I've had a bad day," I said. "My lunch was two hours late and now it's three hours past my usual dinnertime."

"Not ours," he said. "Sheila, tell them to add another dinner like the ones we ordered. There'll be three of us." He looked at me. "Filet. Okay?"

"Fine," I said. "I apologize for being rude to your inoffensive wife."

He smiled. Aunt Sheila said, "Slowly now. Don't crowd your luck."

I ignored her. I leaned back and told Homer about my day right through my visit with Dawn Rhodes.

"Dawn Rhodes," he said, and shook his head. "I never liked her much. Always stirring up trouble. A regular Drew Pearson."

"You'd love her if you met her," I said. "So now we come to the Village Sanitarium. If I hope to learn what I want to up there, it might cost money."

Our beer came and Aunt Sheila brought it over. Homer

sipped his and asked, "What did you hope to learn up there?"

"The picture. Which would lead me to Rivali's killer."

Homer said, "I wouldn't pay five cents to find out who killed Rivali. Did you plan to bribe somebody up at this quacks' roost?"

"If that's the only way I can do it and if even that is possible."

"Aren't you sure Rivali killed Mary Mae?"

I shook my head. "And even if I was, I'd still want to find out who killed Rivali."

"Why? You wouldn't make a nickel on it. Aren't you in business to make money?"

"Not completely. I hate killers."

"Not all of them," he said soothingly. "Not the public benefactor who bumped off Enrico Rivali."

"If I don't hate the killer, I still hate the act," I said. "You don't want to spend any more money, eh, Homer?"

"I don't want to be responsible," he said, "for bringing the killer of Enrico Rivali to the unjust law. Hell, man, he might get thirty days." He winked. "That's a joke, son."

"Not to me," I said. "Death *never* is, to me."

From the background, where she had been unusually quiet, Aunt Sheila said, "Brock's right, Homer."

He winked at me and didn't answer.

"After all," Aunt Sheila said, "to use your line, Homer Gallup, *it's only money!*"

"That was before we were married," he said. "I was trying to impress you." He shook his head. "I don't like it, Brock. Not bribery and not messing into the death of that Rivali."

Aunt Sheila started to say something and stopped. I didn't even start to say anything. There hadn't been any noticeable change in the tone of Homer's voice but he had made it clear that his decision was firm. The executive touch. . . .

We weren't strained at dinner but there was an absence of the jovial hilarity our other meetings had engendered. We were polite and friendly and I was embarrassed.

I had come to Homer with a suggestion that he invest more in this investigation than my day wages. If he wanted to, he could read that as an attempt of his wife's nephew to milk some extra money out of him.

At ten-thirty, I said, "I have to go. Thanks for the fine meal."

Homer asked, "How about some golf tomorrow? I'm getting sick of sitting around."

"I have to go up to Camarillo," I said. "How about the day after tomorrow?"

"Camarillo?" He stared at me. "On your own time? Why?"

"A man is dead. Why not?"

"Oh, Jesus!" he said. "What kind of man?"

"Homer," I said patiently, "I can't explain it to you if you don't think as I do. And if you did, I wouldn't have to explain it."

"All right!" he said impatiently. "How much, how much?"

"Not a penny, Homer. It's just a whim of mine. Good night."

He looked doubtfully at Aunt Sheila but she made no comment. He said, "Good night. Be careful, won't you?"

I nodded and went out and down the short flight of steps to the lobby and out to the portico. There, an attendant asked, "May I get your car, sir?"

"Get your own goddamned car," I told him. "I'm a poor man."

I walked down below the sky-high palms to my tired flivver. The engine started with a clatter and I drove down the winding drive, past the portico and the attendant, down to Sunset and the ten-thirty traffic, mostly Cads.

Resentment led nowhere; I tried to think of something pleasant. I thought of Jan and was more depressed. I thought of Joyce Thorne. I thought of the Sunday afternoon I had nailed Frankie Albert for a thirty-seven-yard loss when he'd gone back to pass.

At home, my little nest smelled musty. I opened all the windows and made myself a pot of coffee. I sat up for two hours, plotting my tomorrow.

In the morning, Aunt Sheila phoned. "Homer's embarrassed," she told me.

"There's no reason to be," I said, "and I don't want his money. You've been talking to him, haven't you?"

"I swear to you I have not. He's embarrassed all by himself. He thinks he has let down his finest California friend."

"You tell him we're still friends," I said. "I think he's an ace."

"I think he's a deuce this morning," she said. "Now, you be careful, Rockhead Callahan."

I promised her I would. I asked her to forward my regards to Jan. Then I made my own breakfast and headed for the Valley, via Sepulveda.

The Valley was hot this spring morning. The freeway turned into Ventura Boulevard and then turned into a freeway again, and we were skimming along between the green hills.

Only in the spring is it really green in this end of the state, but it was beautiful this morning. The smog was behind and we were back in California. Los Angeles is not California, not in any way. Los Angeles is a fungus that will some day destroy California.

There is a mental hospital at Camarillo and the rumor I had was that the physician who now headed the Village Sanitarium had formerly been on the staff of this hospital but had been forced to resign. By persons and for reasons unknown. To laymen.

He hadn't been the founder of the Village Sanitarium. That doubtful honor went to a man named Newton, a man without any acceptable medical degree, who had died at the age of sixty-three, only eighteen months ago, stabbed to death by a betrayed husband of twenty-six. At sixty-three, killed by a young and betrayed husband. . . . It wasn't exactly admirable; why did I admire him?

In the washed, clear air, the hills seemed greener now and the sky was an impossible blue. Why did I live in Los Angeles? Why did I continue to reside in that middle-brow, low-class saucer of smog, when all these green hills were within reach?

Because I had to eat, that's why. Because all my clients came from the tarnished or troubled people, and Los Angeles had a surplus of those.

To the right of the road, enormous signs heralded the birth of a new country club. And also view lots and luxury homes that would encircle the golf course and which would entitle the buyer to membership. The luxury homes could be purchased for as little as three thousand dollars down. There was no explanation given as to why a man with only three thousand dollars should think he was entitled to a luxury home and a golf-club membership.

Forge on, America, into the atomic age. Armed only with a putter. . . .

I forged on, the flivver chirping healthily, now that she could breathe. At a side road, a mile short of the Camarillo turnoff, I turned toward the hills.

The Village Sanitarium was a full two miles from the Camarillo Hospital, an establishment occupying about five acres in a grove of eucalyptus and live oak on the sunny side of the slope.

The main building was white stucco and varnished redwood; the outer buildings were cottages of redwood, smothered in scarlet bougainvillaea. The pool was imitation white marble, Olympic size.

Here a drunk could be dried out, an alcoholic temporarily arrested, a narcotics addict weaned, and (if properly credited and financially certified) an heir could be aborted. Here, the mentally sick who should be in Camarillo could be made even sicker (and poorer) by the suave and inept staff.

At least this is what I had been told.

I parked the flivver between a Jaguar and a Bentley on the cool, tree-shaded parking lot and walked thoughtfully up to the entrance of the main building.

The lobby was dim and colorfully furnished, doors leading off it bearing the names of the staff. A pleasant, white-haired lady sat behind a maple desk in here.

"Good morning," she said. "Have you come to visit someone?"

"No, ma'am. I came to see Dr. Carlson. My name is Brock Callahan." I showed her a photostat of my license.

"A private detective?" she asked doubtfully.

"Very private," I assured her. "Dr. Carlson has nothing to fear from me. I come only for information."

She frowned and took a deep breath.

I asked, "Did you serve under Mr. Newton too?"

"I worked under Dr. Newton," she admitted. "Why do you ask?"

"I just wondered. I didn't know he was an M.D."

"I didn't *say* he was an M.D.," she replied. "Though Dr. Carlson is."

"Still is eh?" I shook my head in wonder. "What county is this you're in?"

She took another breath. "Mr. Callahan, your attitude makes me doubt that you're here for any good purpose. Would you mind telling me what it is?"

"Information," I said. "On a former patient. A woman

by the name of Mary Mae Milgrim.''

The old girl seemed to wince and her eyes were sad for a moment. "Mary Mae," she said quietly. "Mary Mae Milgrim. That's horrible, what happened to Mary Mae Milgrim."

"It was," I agreed. "Could I see Dr. Carlson now?"

"Why? He wasn't here when—" She broke off abruptly and began to blush. "I mean, he's never had any contact with Miss Milgrim."

"What you meant to say was that the doctor wasn't here when Mary Mae was. Were you?"

She lifted her chin and said firmly. "There are no records here of anyone named Mary Mae Milgrim ever having been a patient."

"There had better be," I said.

She stared at me anxiously.

"A sweet girl like that," I went on, "murdered so horribly, and here could be the information to convict her killer, and you sit there and tell me there are no records."

"I'm telling you the truth."

"In your mind, there's a record," I said. "Are you a human being or aren't you?"

She stared at me, her face red, her chin quivering.

A door opened and a man almost as big as I asked, "Everything all right, Miss Cornelius?"

"Why shouldn't it be?" I asked him. "Go back into your hole."

"It's—a private detective, Dr. Carlson." Miss Cornelius told the big man. "He's seeking information on Mary Mae Milgrim."

"And who," he asked coolly, "is Mary Mae Milgrim?"

Miss Cornelius said nothing. She stared at the top of her desk.

Dr. Carlson looked sharply at me. "Do you want to leave now, quietly, or shall we call the sheriff?"

"I want you to call the sheriff," I said. "I'll wait right here." I went over and sat in a maple pull-up chair. I picked up a copy of *Newsweek*.

Miss Cornelius said, "It was—before your time, Doctor. It was years and years ago."

"And the records?"

"They were destroyed in that fire we had eight years ago," she said softly.

He said, "All right, mister, what more do you want."

"The sheriff," I said. "I'll wait."

"Why?" he asked. "Have we been unco-operative?"

"Yes." I looked at him levelly. "Miss Cornelius has admitted Miss Milgrim was here by speaking of the records being destroyed. I'd like a quiet talk with Miss Cornelius."

"You'll go," he said. "Right now." He paused. "Or I'll call a couple of our bigger attendants to put you out."

"Call 'em," I said. I reached under my jacket and took out my .38, holding it lightly in my hand.

A startled exclamation came from Miss Cornelius. Dr. Carlson moved nervously toward the door behind him, staring at the gun in my hand.

"Call the sheriff," I said. "Call him now and we'll get everything ironed out. Maybe you ought to call the County Medical Board at the same time."

Carlson licked his lips and said softly, "That was a highly irrational action, mister. That—"

"My name is Callahan," I told him. "Brock Callahan. You can call any of a dozen chiefs of police in this end of the state if you'd like a report on my integrity or rationality. This .38 was simply protection against the voiced threat of your underpaid and overweight attendants. I didn't come here for violence. You were the first to suggest it."

He frowned. "Callahan—? Brock, did you say?"

"I remember you," Miss Cornelius said. "You played with the Dodgers."

"Not quite, ma'am. Are we going to talk or fight?"

Miss Cornelius said primly. "We aren't going to do anything until you put that gun back where you got it from. A big man like you, an athlete, waving a gun like some juvenile—"

I gazed at her in candid admiration. She had regained the dominance while the big slob behind her was still quaking. I put the gun back and bowed in surrender.

She turned in her chair. "Dr. Carlson, none of this will be or can be connected with you. I'll talk with Mr. Callahan on my lunch hour."

"Fine," he said. "Fine." He went back into his office and quickly closed the door.

Miss Cornelius told me, "It's a little restaurant called The Fireside. It's on the south side of the road, just on the limits of Oak City." She looked at her watch. "Oak City is about half a mile down this road we're on. I should be there in half an hour."

FIFTEEN

THE FIRESIDE WAS an exceptionally attractive spot for a rural restaurant. It had a fairly large, circular dining room, all tables within view of the mammoth fireplace of fieldstone. It had a small bar in a separate room, cool and quiet.

It had a small bartender too, a bald, thin gentleman with an Irish face and a mellow voice. He didn't have Einlicher, but he had High Life, which is the next best

As he poured it, he said, "You wouldn't be the Rock, would you?"

I nodded, and held out a hand.

"I thought I recognized you," he said, "My name is Joe Nolan. What was the matter with our boys last fall?"

"Nothing," I said. "The opposition was better. Every year it gets to be a tougher league."

"I guess," he said. "Up here on business?"

"With Miss Cornelius," I agreed. "Know her?"

"Kitty? Everybody around here knows Kitty. Wonderful girl to be working at an abortion mill like that Sanitarium. Yet she's been there thirty-five years." He paused. "You know, maybe it would be a *worse* place if Kitty wasn't there."

"Maybe," I agreed.

"And I suppose," he went on, "that some of them imitation religions don't consider abortion as murder, probably not even a sin, huh?''

"Imitation religions?" I asked.

"Protestant," he explained. "Don't tell me you're a left-handed Irishman?"

"I—uh—haven't been to Mass lately," I admitted.

His pale blue eyes looked at me accusingly. "Why not?"

"Let's not fight, Joe," I said. "Tell me more about Kitty."

Some of the warmth had left the room. "You're a private eye now, right?"

I nodded.

"You planning some trouble for Kitty Cornelius?"

"Never. She's going to give me some information. Is Miss Cornelius Catholic?"

"Naw. Her old lady was a Swede and her pa half German. Kitty's all right, though, even if she works at that place. The kids she's helped around here—" He poured half a glass of beer and sipped it. "Don't you ever think about dying?"

"Frequently."

"And aren't you scared, when you think about it?"

"Usually."

"Then why don't you go to Mass?"

"Joe," I said, "you go, and I'll bet you don't want to die either."

"That's different," he said. "You wait, Callahan, you wait 'til the time comes. You'll be sorry."

"Probably," I agreed, and then Miss Kitty was there and I went out to sit at a table with her in a corner of the dining room.

She ordered a whiskey sour and I ordered another beer and we studied the luncheon menu.

Then she put the menu down and said, "You certainly flexed your muscles back there, didn't you?"

"It seemed to be the time for it," I said.

"I'm not criticizing," she said. "I can understand it. I'm Irish, myself."

"Only one fourth," I corrected her.

Her eyes widened. "Now who told you that?" She looked toward the barroom. "Oh, I suppose— Well, anyway, I like to think of myself as Irish."

"Why are we sparring?" I asked her. "Did you change your mind? Did you decide not to tell me about Mary Mae?"

She looked at the linen on the table. "Mary Mae was a sweet, sweet girl and now she's dead. What good can it do to go digging into her history?"

"If it wouldn't do any good, I wouldn't be here. Miss Cornelius, you have to trust me. I don't reveal any scandal unless it has to be done. I have never willfully damaged anyone's reputation."

She said nothing, looking at her whiskey sour.

I asked, "Did Mary Mae come there for an abortion?"

Without looking at me, she nodded.

"And then changed her mind?"

She nodded again, and looked up at me. "I—talked her out of it. I've—talked a number of them out of it. That's why I stay there, year after year."

"Couldn't you do better by reporting them?"

"Could I? If an abortion will save a life, it's legal. And there are any number of doctors in Los Angeles who will diagnose an abortion as life-saving."

"Couldn't the State Medical Board do something?"

"I suppose. So then, all the girls who were determined to have abortions would go to men even less qualified. Or the button hook witches. My God, some of the places—" She sipped her drink.

The waitress came, and we ordered. Kitty Cornelius said, "You didn't come up here to get the lowdown on the sanitarium racket, I'm sure. This much I'll tell you—Mary

Mae had her baby and it was a healthy baby. That's all I
can tell you because it's all I know.''

"She wasn't married at the time?''

"Of course not. You know that. She never married.''

"Why not?''

"How do I know? I didn't marry because nobody worthwhile ever asked me. Maybe that was her problem too.''

"It couldn't have been,'' I said. "Millions of men must
have loved her.''

"How many million does it take, though, to find *one
worthwhile man?* Don't tell me about men, Callahan; I've
had more experience with their evil doings than you have.''

"Kitty,'' I said, "you malign us.''

"You're not married,'' she said. "Why not?''

"Because my true love won't have me.''

"Get another then. There are a lot more worthwhile
women than men in this world, you can be damned sure of
that.''

"Kitty,'' I said, "what you need is another whiskey
sour.''

She shook her head.

I asked, "Who paid for the abortion that Mary Mae didn't
get?''

She shook her head. "I don't know. But you can be sure
he had money, the way Dr. Frank Newton used to charge.
I never handled the books.''

Our lunches came and we ate without any further informa-
tive dialogue. Her whole life, she told me, had been spent
within ten miles of this restaurant where we sat; she was
one of those rare creatures, a native Californian.

"Do you get into Los Angeles much?'' I asked her.

"I used to,'' she said. "Not lately. It's turning into a
horrible town, isn't it?''

"Noisy, dirty and evil-smelling,'' I admitted, "but it has
its offbeat charm, too. This rural life can get dull, can't it?''

"Not at the Village Sanitarium. Maybe, if I didn't have that, I'd be happy to join your ratrace, Callahan."

"It's quite often depressing," I told her, "but it's never dull. Kitty, think back, try to remember if there isn't something you can tell me that will point a finger at the murderer."

She finished her coffee. "I've been thinking ever since I read about Miss Milgrim in the paper. And all I can remember is what I've already told you. And now I have to get back to my repulsive work."

"You're a saint," I told her, "a saint in hell. If you ever need a strong arm, I hope you'll think of me."

I left her there and went out to the flivver. A huge sign across the street advertised lots for sale in "Smog-free, secluded, pastoral Oak City—Exceptional investment opportunities—"

Through the windows of the barroom, I could see Joe Nolan's disapproving eyes and I waved, but he didn't wave back. I opened the windows in my hot car and turned west toward Highway 101.

Peaceful and pastoral this area might be, but I had a hunch it would drive me nuts. People were sickening but I had to have them around; I needed them.

My psychic flivver snorted in derision; she can read my thoughts and usually holds them in contempt. We had been together a long time. I was much more tolerant with her than she with me.

Mary Mae, Mary Mae, Mary Mae. . . . So now the pattern was forming, the events leading up to the act were coming into focus. But to what avail? Mary Mae would be just as dead. And would solving this murder stay some other murderer's hand? Perhaps, though it was doubtful.

Today, I wasn't even being paid. Today, I was working in the interest of justice.

The sun was out in all its glory now and heat waves shimmered off the road. We were going steadily uphill on a long seven-per-cent grade and the speedometer needle kept dropping. This was quite a grind for my old girl.

At the top, we were down to forty, and ahead of us now, and below us, was the San Fernando Valley, the fastest growing area in the world. A yellow layer of smog hung over it to the horizon.

I cut off the Ventura Freeway onto Sepulveda and cut off that on Wilshire, heading for the ocean.

In an area of small homes, in Santa Monica, I walked past the larger house on the front of the lot to the smaller home in the rear. The flowers were still there.

And Blanche Arden Thorne was spraying her roses. She turned and smiled as I came up. I thought it was an uncertain smile.

"It's too late for lunch," she said. "I've already had it. A beer?"

"No, thanks. Herbie around?"

"He's playing golf," she said. She set the sprayer down carefully and went over to wash her hands at a hose tap. "Damned aphids," she said.

I sat on a redwood bench and waited for her to turn around.

She stood up, dried her hands on a rag and came over to sit quietly on the bench on the other side of the table. She finally looked at me.

I said, "I've just come from the Village Sanitarium. Do you know where it is?"

"I've heard of it."

"You knew Mary Mae better than anyone. You knew all about her. You didn't tell me she'd been up there."

Her voice was dull. "What business was it of yours?"

"You were her best friend," I went on. "In all the world, you were her closest friend."

"Probably," she admitted.

"But she didn't leave you her money, did she?"

"I don't know. If she did, I haven't been informed."

"She didn't."

Blanche Arden Thorne shrugged and said nothing.

"Should we start over?" I asked. "Should we start with the truth, for a change?"

"You're not a police officer," she said.

"Shall I get one, and then we can start over?"

"Go ahead," she said defiantly. "Get one. And I'll tell him I don't know who killed Mary Mae Milgrim. And that's all he's got a right to ask me, isn't it? He can't ask me about things that happened thirty years ago, can he?"

"He can ask," I said, "but I can tell him that. I'm trying to do this my way, Mrs. Thorne. I'm trying to keep the lambs from being hurt and still catch the wolf. The police haven't time to worry about the lambs. And the newspapers then have a field day with the lambs."

"Don't threaten me," she said quietly.

"Believe me, I'm not. I'm explaining my position and why it would be best all around for you to confide in me. I have a certain right to privacy so long as it doesn't interfere with justice. I can use it to help the innocents."

"But you wouldn't," she said. "I was in the industry for twenty-five years, Mr. Callahan. Don't you think, in that time, I learned about men like you, scandalmongers, Peeping Toms?"

"I'm not one of those," I said, "and you know it. I can give you any number of first-class references."

She said nothing, staring at her flowers.

"Two are already dead," I said. "A vein of violence has been brought into life. The first murder is always the hardest one; a killer gets hardened quickly after that."

"The murderer is dead," she said. "We know that. You know that."

"Who murdered him?"

She continued to look at her flowers. "What does it matter, who murdered Enrico Rivali? His death was long overdue."

I swore and she looked up, startled. I said, "How do you develop that kind of callousness—by spraying roses, by planting marigolds? Is that how you build up a stomach for *murder?*"

She looked at the ground.

"You didn't call me a scandalmonger the first time I came here," I went on. "Why do you want to hate me now? So you don't have to hate yourself?"

She continued to look at the ground.

I stood up. "All right. I'll go get a police officer. You've withheld information and they consider that the same as a lie. I'm sick of trying to protect the innocent."

She looked up and her look was doubtful. She said, "Is this another threat?"

I shook my head.

She said, "Mary Mae is dead and nothing can bring her back. Enrico is dead and nobody will cry. Nothing more is going to happen. You know that. That corny pitch about a 'a vein of violence,' you know that's nonsense. It's the kind of excuse people like you use in order to—" She broke off, staring past me.

My peasant prescience made the hair tingle at the back of my neck. I was almost afraid to turn around, to see what she was staring at.

But I did.

It was George Parkas, coming across the grass toward us, a big old Western six-shooter in his shaking hand.

≈≈≈≈≈≈≈≈≈ *SIXTEEN* ≈≈≈≈≈≈≈≈≈≈

BLANCHE ARDEN THORNE opened her mouth wide, but no sound came out.

Parkas said, "Nobody hollers and maybe nobody gets hurt. Answers, that's all I want. From Callahan."

George was nervous but that didn't make me fear him any less. He was nervous enough to pull the trigger on that old Colt without actually meaning to.

"What kind of answers, George?" I asked quietly.

"Who got Enrico, that's what I want to know."

"I'm trying to find out," I said patiently. "My client left me yesterday, because he wasn't interested, so I'm trying to find out on my own time, in the interest of justice."

"Huh!" he said. "You lying bastard!"

"Call my client," I told him. "Do you have a permit for that gun, George?"

"My name is Mr. Parkas, to you," he said.

Blanche Arden Thorne said shakily, "Mr. Callahan is telling the truth. He really is trying to find out who killed Mr. Rivali."

George's ugly face hardened as he stared at her. "Oh? And he came here to find out? Why here?"

There was a silence. The gun was probably a prop used by George when he played heavies. I wondered if it was loaded with something besides blank cartridges. There was a way to find out, but I didn't feel lucky.

"Why here?" he repeated. "Come on, somebody better start talking damned quick."

I thought I heard a sound from the house and I glanced that way. Luckily, George was looking at Blanche and didn't notice my glance. For Herbie had come home from golf, his bag over his shoulder. He stood on the back porch, taking it all in.

I said quickly, "I'll tell you what I can, Mr. Parkas. And perhaps you can fill in the rest." I moved slightly to my right, and he turned to keep the gun pointed at my belly.

Now his back was to the house, and I began slowly. "It occurred to me, when I learned that Mr. Rivali and Miss Thorne were to share in the inheritance of Mary Mae Milgrim—"

Herbie had taken one club from his bag, a wood. It looked like his driver, a heavy club, with a big face. Blanche saw him, looked startled for a second—and then interrupted me to attract George's attention.

"That isn't quite right, Mr. Callahan. I understand that Joyce is the sole heir."

"Originally," I said slowly, "both Joyce and Mr. Rivali were to split Miss Milgrim's estate evenly, but her attorney told me just the other day that—"

Herbie was coming quietly along the grass. He wasn't holding the club high, but over to his right side, as though he meant to deliver a lateral rather than a downward blow. I hoped and prayed that he was a low handicapper.

"—and so," I went on, "it seemed logical to me that Mr. Rivali believed one of two things. Either he was still an heir or Miss Joyce Thorne had cheated him out of his share by—"

Herbie was within range now, and the driver was way around to the right. His left arm was bowed only a little, his grip and stance were adjusted only enough to permit an upward sweeping blow rather than a downward sweeping blow.

It was a horrible weapon and my voice faltered and George was instantly suspicious.

Luckily, Herbie started to swing before George turned around. Or George would have lost his entire face. For it was an extremely broad and deep-faced driver and Herbie swung like a champion.

It was a direct hit over George's ear and it sounded like a heavy watermelon cracking open on a concrete road.

The matron came into the room and said, "We've given Mrs. Thorne a sedative. She kept mumbling something about a 'vein of violence,' whatever that means."

Captain McHugh looked at Herbie and Herbie shrugged. Captain McHugh looked at me.

I said, "I used the phrase in talking about Rivali's death."

This was Santa Monica headquarters and I am not really appreciated in Santa Monica. Captain McHugh said, "Mrs. Thorne is in shock. But you two don't look any the worse for wear. Used to this kind of sight, are you?"

"Almost," I said. "The sound made me sick, and then I stopped looking. Will he live?"

Captain McHugh shrugged and looked at Herbie. Herbie said, "He had a gun pointed at my wife. If it happened again I'd do just what I did again."

"I thought the gun was pointing at Callahan," McHugh said.

"Most of the time," I admitted. "But Mr. Thorne couldn't make that distinction from where he stood."

McHugh frowned and looked at my statement. "You say here that you warned Captain Devine over at the West Los Angeles Station about this Parkas yesterday. You said he was dangerous. He hasn't any record to support that assumption."

"He was dangerous yesterday. His—best friend, hell— his *sweetheart* had been murdered. And he's a violent man. I think it would be obvious to anyone but young Captain Devine that he should have been held."

McHugh smiled briefly. "He didn't impress you, eh?"

"Not for a second."

"Sweetheart? What did you mean by that crack?"

"Check it," I said. "Call Lieutenant Remington over at Beverly Hills Headquarters."

McHugh looked doubtful.

Herbie said, "Everybody in the industry knew Rivali was queer. And this Parkas was living with him. A guy doesn't need a diagram."

McHugh said sternly, "We don't operate on rumor here, Mr. Thorne."

"You got a town full of 'em," Herbie said belligerently. "If anybody should be able to spot a homo, a Santa Monica cop should."

McHugh stared at him and Herbie stared right back. McHugh said, "I'll tolerate no insolence."

Herbie muttered something and stared at the floor.

McHugh picked up the phone and said, "Get me Lieutenant Remington over at Beverly Hills."

A pause, while he stared out the window at the bay and Herbie lighted a cigarette. Then, "Lieutenant, this is Captain McHugh. There's a man here by the name of Brock Callahan who claims to be working with your Department in the—"

His voice went on and I stared out the window, remembering the sound that driver had made as it crashed into George's skull. Little Herbie Thorne had more stomach than I had. I couldn't do that to anyone, not with a weapon that vicious.

McHugh finished talking and replaced the phone.

"Okay, Callahan, you can go." He said to Herbie, "I

suppose you'll want to wait until you're sure your wife is ready to travel? She's probably still in shock.''

Herbie nodded.

"We can talk while we're waiting," Captain McHugh explained. "So long, Callahan."

"So long, Captain," I said. "Thank you for your courtesy." I left him on that ironic note.

It was four o'clock, too early for dinner after my full lunch. There would be no percentage in talking with the elder Thornes in their present state. I headed for Beverly Hills.

Joyce Thorne opened the door to her rent-free cottage and stared at me coldly. She offered no word of greeting.

I said, "I've just left your parents, over at Santa Monica Police Headquarters. They had a—rather bad scare."

Her eyes widened. "What happened? Is this a trick—?"

"No, Miss Thorne. Why would I trick you?"

"Are they all right?"

I nodded.

"Come in," she said. "What happened?"

I came in and said, "It's a long story. It starts a few years back. What happened this afternoon was that Rivali's friend, George Parkas, threatened your mother and me with a gun. Your dad came home from golf, sneaked up behind George with a golf club and removed the threat."

"He didn't—?"

"Kill him? Not yet. It's touch and go. Do you have any beer in the place? It's been a hot day."

She hesitated, staring at me.

"I'm not going to crowd you," I said. "You can tell me only what you want to and I imagine that will be nothing. I'm working on my own time and thought I was working to protect you. I'm not sure, now, that I'll even continue working at all."

She paused, and then went to the kitchen. From here, she called, "Do you prefer to drink directly from the can?"

"Please," I called back.

She brought me one of the new pint cans, what the brewer labels as "half-quart" can. It was cold and almost as good as High Life, though far short of Einlicher.

"Why don't you sit down?" she asked. "This isn't a bar."

I sat in an upholstered chair and smiled at her. She sat on the davenport and asked, "What did you mean about my telling you only what I want to? Do you think I've been lying to you?"

"I wouldn't call it lying. I think you've been withholding information, probably."

I sipped the cold, wet beer and shrugged.

"You're not making sense," she said.

"Perhaps not. I'm enjoying the beer. It's been a—a tiring day. And seeing a man's head cracked with a driver is sort of unsettling. Give me a few minutes."

She lighted a cigarette and stared moodily at the big bank of windows. I sipped the beer and tried to relax.

Finally she said impatiently, "Name one lie that I've told you, just *one!*"

I finished the beer. "When you phoned that morning, you told me that Miss Milgrim was in desperate need of money."

"That was on Miss Milgrim's orders. You know that isn't what I meant. Point out one lie I've told you since the—since Miss Milgrim died."

I smiled. "You told my uncle I was measuring the moat."

"You're impossible," she said. "Impossible!"

"All right," I said wearily, "I withdraw the charge. And I'll ask you quite humbly if there is anything you want to tell me now?"

She picked at her dress, her eyes downcast. "I've learned,

since last we talked, that I'm the sole heir to Miss Milgrim's estate.''

''Haven't you wondered why?''

She looked up to stare at me. ''Should I? I assumed it was another of her temporary whims. She was a woman with an iron whim. Should I wonder why?''

''Your mother was her best friend.'' I paused. ''Not you.''

There was honest bewilderment in Joyce's eyes. ''Did she have a fight with Mother? Is that what you're trying to say? Or that scandal Rivali talked about, did that concern Mother?''

I shook my head.

Her voice shook. '':Why are you being so cryptic? Do you like to torment me?''

''Of course not,'' I said softly.

The phone rang, and she went to answer it. I heard her say, ''Oh, Dad—are you all right? And Mother? Oh, thank God. I've been so worried since Mr. Callahan—yes, he's here now.'' A long pause. ''Of course, if you want to. Dad, what's the secret?'' A pause. ''Oh, all right!''

She came into the living room to tell me, ''My dad wants to speak with you.''

I went in and picked up the phone and Herbie Thorne said quietly, ''She doesn't know, Mr. Callahan. Not unless you've told her.''

''I haven't.''

''Are you going to?''

''Not unless I have to.''

A pause. ''Look, Blanche and I, we've saved a few dollars and I know you fellows have a rough go of it and we thought—''

''Mr. Thorne,'' I told him firmly, ''I'm always for rent but never for sale. I'll do what I can to protect everybody who deserves it and that's all I can promise you.''

''That's why you didn't tell Captain McHugh,'' he said.

"Blanche and I, we thought maybe you didn't tell him because—Well, we were wrong. I sure hope you can keep it quiet, Mr. Callahan."

"I'll try to. That's all I can promise."

I replaced the phone and came back to the living room. Joyce Thorne stared at me angrily. "Secrets, secrets, secrets! Am I too young to know? My mother was in the picture business for years, Mr. Callahan. I never expected that she was a saint."

"None of us are," I said. "Is there anything you want to tell me before I leave?"

"It's your turn," she said. "You tell me. Whatever it is, I'll find out, so why don't you tell me now?"

"I'm not free to," I said. "I'm still a *private* detective."

≋≋≋≋≋≋≋≋ *SEVENTEEN* ≋≋≋≋≋≋≋≋

I LEFT HER with her doubts and went over to Beverly Hills Headquarters. Remington was still there, in his office.

He told me, "Gnup just phoned from the hospital. Parkas thinks he's going to die and he's spilling his guts. It was Rivali who killed Mary Mae, just as we thought."

"Why?"

"She'd threatened to change her will. He'd been blackmailing her for years about some old scandal, and she finally got fed up and told him she was cutting him out of her will."

"He didn't know she already had?"

"Evidently not."

"Did Parkas know what Rivali was blackmailing Mary Mae about? Did he know what the scandal was?"

Remington shook his head. "But we can guess, can't we? She never married, did she? And people like Parkas and Rivali would be quick to spot another of their kind, wouldn't they?"

I said nothing, thinking of Kitty Cornelius and the Thornes.

"You don't look convinced," Remington said. "Maybe you have another theory?"

"I was wondering who killed Rivali. Aren't you?"

"We think it's suicide. Is anybody paying you to investigate Rivali's death?"

"No. My client pulled out last night."

He stared at me. "Well, then, what the hell do you care who killed Rivali?"

I said evenly, "The State was kind enough to license me. In simple reciprocation, I figure I owe it to the State to be a citizen."

He continued to stare. "You have to be kidding."

Anger moved in me.

"Don't glower," he said. "I withdraw the sneer. Callahan, what gnaws you, what drives you?"

"Nothing. I'm an adjusted man. But what's wrong with wanting an orderly case and an orderly world?"

He sat quietly for seconds. "You know something, don't you?"

I stared at him, neither denying nor affirming.

He asked, "Where were you this morning?"

"I took a drive in my flivver. I wanted to get out of the smog for half a day."

"You're not co-operating," he said.

"On what, a closed case? If I catch a killer before I hit the hay tonight, I'll bring him in. Simply as a gesture from a public-spirited citizen. My reports to you, Lieutenant, ended with yesterday's. Because the case we worked on together is closed." I started to leave.

"Just a second," he said.

I turned to stare at him.

"If you know something, Callahan, we want it."

"When I know something," I said, "you'll get it. So long, Lieutenant."

I went home. I took a shower and read the *Times* I hadn't had time to read this morning, all the glowing tributes to the great genius of Enrico Rivali. The people who were writing about him were sincere; Rivali was their kind of man. He was their brother, another jackal from the same pack.

*Don't be bitter, Callahan. You had three days' work.
You are still alive and healthy. Who wants to live in a perfect
world?*

I opened two cans of beefburger soup and ate half a loaf
of rye bread with it. The sun went down and the traffic
began to diminish; I climbed into the groaning flivver and
headed for Hollywood.

In the weathered building on Kenmore, John Davenport
opened his door and said, "Well, Mr. Callahan. Come in."

I came into the room that held the studio couch, the
wooden card table, the coffee table made from a piano bench
and all the photographs on the walls.

"What have you been doing?" he asked me.

I sat in one of the frayed easy chairs. "I've been reading
the columns of Dawn Rhodes."

He sat on the piano bench and stared at me. "Is she still
writing somewhere?"

I shook my head. "I've been reading her old columns,
down in the *Times* morgue."

"She was the best," he said. "What else have you been
doing?"

"Oh, I took a little trip up to the Village Sanitarium. Do
you know where that is? It's near Camarillo."

"I know where it is," he said. "Would you like a drink?"

"I don't drink. Don't let me stop you."

He went over and poured a drink of the Scotch I'd brought
him. He came back to sit on the piano bench.

I looked at the picture of Mary Mae. To *stubborn and
gifted John Davenport*. I said, "When she called you stubborn, she was referring to the fact that you wouldn't marry
her, wasn't she?"

"I suppose," he admitted. "Why are you here, Mr. Callahan?"

"To talk," I said. "She was quite a girl, wasn't she?
Loved one man all her adult life. You."

He shrugged. "It's possible. Stranger things have happened."

"Never married," I went on. "Was true to you all her life. Had a child by you, a daughter. Had it secretly, because in those days that kind of scandal would have destroyed her."

He raised a hand. "I want to explain about that. She told me she'd had an abortion. Until two nights ago, I had no idea I had a daughter in this world."

"Joyce Thorne, that's your daughter. Joyce Thorne, brought up by Blanche Arden, because Blanche was married."

He nodded again. "What started you thinking about Joyce?"

"The inheritance. Blanche was the friend, not Joyce. Joyce had to be closer, if she was inheriting. About the only way to be closer was to be a relative, a *close* relative."

He sighed and sipped his Scotch.

"What did Rivali want?" I asked him.

"The first time—" he paused—"I mean, *that* time?"

"You meant the *first* time," I corrected him. "The second time he came, you killed him. And then drove him in his car to his house and left him there. There'll be prints in that car, don't worry. They're probably looking for someone to match them to, right now."

He stared at the floor. He belched.

"The first time," he said, after a second, "he had one of his complicated schemes for blackmailing Joyce and getting enough money from her and possibly from Mr. Gallup to finance a picture, which he would direct and in which I would have a fat part."

"Why Mr. Gallup?"

"I don't know. There's no connection between him and Joyce, but Rivali could keep a lot of irons in the fire at one time without getting burned. He was a—moral juggler. And that night, with you outside, he told me Joyce Thorne was my daughter. It was a—a horrible shock. And then, well, damn it—I was suddenly kind of—proud. A daughter, a child. My only child."

He sipped his drink, staring at the faded carpeting on the floor.

"Go on," I prompted him.

"Then we all went down to Headquarters," he said, "and went through that—that official farce, and then you brought me home. And I couldn't sleep. Damn it, I kept thinking of that girl, my daughter, threatened by a bastard like Rivali. What could it do to her, learning she was illegitimate?"

"And you phoned Rivali?"

John Davenport shook his head slowly. "The son of a bitch came here."

"Why? At that time of night? He was released at two o'clock."

"That's what I asked myself. If we were going to blackmail Joyce, what was the hurry? I realized he must have some other reason for coming, though he wouldn't voice it, of course. The heat was on, understand? The law was getting closer and closer to Enrico Rivali." He took a breath and looked at his empty glass.

"Pour another," I said. "The night's young."

He went over, poured another, and came back to the piano bench-coffee table-sitter on. "While we were talking, my phone rang. It's there, in the kitchen. He sat in that chair over there, out of my sight from the kitchen. But next to it, see, is that tobacco stand, and if I'm facing the right way in the kitchen, I can see that."

"I understand," I said. "Go on."

"Now, who in hell would call me at almost three o'clock in the morning?"

"George Parkas?" I asked.

He glanced doubtfully at me. "You knew?"

"No. But I'm getting a pattern."

"So did I," he said. "With anyone else, I wouldn't have looked for a pattern—but Rivali? He never made an uncalculated move in his life." He sipped his Scotch. "I glanced toward the living room and all I could see was that tobacco stand, that and Rivali's hand as he put something into the stand and closed the little door again."

"Planting the coniine on you," I said. "The heat was on and he needed a fall guy, and who more logical than the father of the heiress?"

"That's right. He'd be a big help to the police then, wouldn't he? Telling them about the Village Sanitarium, about me, about the Thornes. He'd be a stinking hero, wouldn't he?"

"If he got away with it. What did Parkas claim to want?"

"He wanted to know if Rivali was here and if he could talk with him. And I did some quick thinking. I said Rivali wasn't here, but I'd have him call as soon as he came."

"Didn't that make Rivali nervous, hearing you say that?"

"I came back into this room and told Rivali that the fewer people who knew we were working together, the better. And somehow I knew that was coniine in that tobacco stand. And who would ever suspect John Davenport had any access to coniine?"

I stared at him and he stared back. He smiled wryly. "Fate helped. He had to use the bathroom. I took the phial out of the tobacco stand while he was in there."

"Deliberate," I said quietly. "I had a thought, I mean a hope—that perhaps you had switched drinks or—"

"That's pretty old stuff, isn't it? Perhaps the DA would fall for it. Say, maybe—?"

"Let me warn you," I said, "that all you say or are about to say has to be repeated by me."

"Not all," he said. "Nobody has to know about Joyce. You'll promise me that, won't you?"

"I can't," I said honestly. "I can only promise to try."

"You will try, won't you?"

"I promise. What I can't understand is how you could convince Rivali you were to be trusted when earlier that night you had told him off?"

He smiled. "Would that be difficult, for a man of my talent?"

"I apologize," I said. "I take it back."

He accepted the apology with a gracious nod. "We talked. And then we had one for the road." He sighed. "Poor Enrico, he never saw the road!"

I stared as my flesh crawled.

"Didn't I warn you," he said, "when you drove me home? Did you think I didn't develop the stomach for *any-thing,* all the years I've spent in this town? I can kill, and make a joke, if the corpse is Enrico Rivali."

I shook my head in wonder and disgust.

"A daughter to be protected?" he went on. "An only child? And the memory of two heart attacks in the last eight months? And where would John Davenport get coniine?"

"Don't try to explain it," I said. "I could never understand it, not if you talked forever."

He nodded. "I wouldn't try to explain it to anyone outside of the industry. Anyone inside wouldn't need an explanation."

I rubbed my neck and he finished his second drink.

He asked, "How do we deal? Is that an insult? I guess Brock Callahan wouldn't come here to sell something, would he?"

"I came to deal," I said. "You go down to the Hollywood Station and confess to the murder of Enrico Rivali. If you do that, I'll do my damnedest to see that Joyce and Blanche and Herbie Thorne are protected. That's my deal."

"How about up there, at the Village Sanitarium?"

I thought of Kitty Cornelius. I said, "Nothing will come

out of there. You can think up some reason why you killed
Rivali. You can make up any damned story you want to, but
I want you to confess.''

''And what's in it for you?'' he asked me. ''I'll believe
it isn't money, but I'd like to know what it is.''

''I don't know,'' I admitted. ''I didn't even get paid for
today's dirty work. Somehow, to me, it's mixed up with
being a citizen. But much smarter people have assured me
I'm wrong.''

He smiled once more. ''I can believe you,'' he said.
''You know, killing Rivali, somehow to me that was mixed
up with being a father and a citizen. Maybe we're both
punchy, eh?''

I stood up and he stood up. He said, ''I haven't a car.''

''I'll drop you off at the Hollywood Station,'' I said.

I dropped him off and drove on, toward Westwood, toward home. Tonight, John Davenport would pay for a moral
lapse of thirty long years ago. Patterns, patterns, patterns. . . .

Tomorrow, Remington would suspect that I had brought
John Davenport to justice and might complain that it would
have been possible to bring him over to Beverly Hills, though
it was another jurisdiction.

But tonight, Lieutenant Remington had washed his hands
of the case and it would have been unjust to bring John
Davenport to him. To hell with Lieutenant Remington.

Abortion is murder and John Davenport had agreed to
that murder thirty years ago. It hadn't come off, but he had
agreed. Tonight, he would pay.

Was the pattern always this clean and just? It would take
some tracing and would indicate, if true, an Overseer. If I
believed in an Overseer, why had I left the church?

To hell with all of them. Except Jan, damn her . . . .

The flivver snorted in disdain and jealousy.

The flivver's headlights illuminated the curb in front of

my apartment house and the little Chev waiting there. Jan's little Chev.

I parked behind and got out. She got out and stared at me in the dim light from the traffic half a block away. "Damn you," she said. "Damn your philandering soul! Where have you been?"

"I just dropped John Davenport off at the Hollywood Station. He killed Enrico Rivali."

"Oh," she said. "Oh—? Let's—go up to your place and talk."

"Talk, talk, talk," I said. "I'm sick of talk!"

"Let's go up, anyway," she said, and her voice was shaky. "Oh, Brock, you bastard—"

She came running, and my arms were open. Tomorrow, we could talk. Tonight, we would communicate.